— GOODREADS

Enemies to lovers is my favorite troupe and this one just rocks it! If you like hate at first site books with convincing plot, great characters, hilarious banter, an uptight heroine, a swoon worthy hero, then please go for it. It was an enjoyable read and I like it a lot!

— GOODREADS

PRAISE FOR MIXED MATCH

This story had humor, heart, and heat and also made me hungry =).

— AMAZON

This is classic chick-lit with beautiful poetic passages and a hero and heroine you can root for. I highly recommend it.

— AMAZON

You know from the very beginning; this is a recipe for disaster without recovery and wonder these two can come out of this unscathed. I enjoyed the premise of this story and the journey to forgiveness and healing.

— MIDNIGHTACE BOOK BAR

I couldn't wait for this book to go live! I had the
opportunity to read an ARC of Mixed Match and I
loved it. There is a perfect balance of romantic
tension, well meaning friends, love on the rise. Add to
that a sexy hot guy and a leading lady with important
decisions to make about her career and her heart and
I couldn't stop reading. I can't wait for the next book
in this series.

— AUTHOR, D.W. MARSHALL

PRAISE FOR MIXED EMOTIONS

I thought this book was a page turner as soon as I
started reading it. If you are looking for a great
romance novel, I'd definitely recommend this one!

— AMAZON

Tastefully done love scenes, just enough tension
between "friends", humor, drama and all the things
that we love when reading romance.

— AMAZON

I just wrapped up Mixed Emotions and Heintzelman
officially has a new fan! This was the perfect mix of
spicy, sweet, and a little bit of heat! Zora and Mike
both are such likable characters and I love the friend-
ship embedded deep into their relationship. I was
drawn in from the beginning, with this being the

easy-going, jovial read I needed this week. I'm a sucker for a friends-to-lovers romance and this hit the spot!

— AMAZON

PRAISE FOR WRAPPED UP IN BEAU

Perfect for the holiday season.

— AMAZON

Perfect if you need a quick respite from holiday stress.

— GOODREADS

ALSO FROM MIA HEINTZELMAN

THE ALL MIXED UP SERIES

(EACH BOOK CAN BE READ AS A STANDALONE)

MIXED SIGNALS

MIXED MATCH

MIXED EMOTIONS

ALL MIXED UP - THE SERIES

STANDALONES

IT'S GOT A RING TO IT - RELEASING 2021

HOLIDAY ROMANCE

WRAPPED UP IN BEAU - NOW IN PAPERBACK!

MARRIED & BRIGHT

MINGLE ALL THE WAY

DARK ROMANCE

DEVASTATED: WASTELANDS ACADEMY BOOK 1

THE STACKS W/A EMMALINE ZANTHI

RUINED: WASTELANDS ACADEMY BOOK 2 - RELEASING 2021

MARRIED & BRIGHT

MIA HEINTZELMAN

LeviLynn

Married
&
Bright

Married & Bright
Copyright © 2020 by Mia Heintzelman

First Levi Lynn Books edition November 2020.

Levi Lynn Books can bring authors to your live event. For more information or to book an event, visit our website at www.miaheintzelman.com.
Editing by Danielle Acee and Danylle Salinas
Cover design and Formatting by Tangled Covers
Manufactured in the United States of America

Cataloguing-in-Publication Data
ISBN 978-1-7359788-3-3 (trade pbk.) | ISBN 978-1-7359788–4-0 (ebook)
Name: Heintzelman, Mia, author.
Title: Married & Bright / Mia Heintzelman
Description: Mia Heintzelman | Las Vegas: Mia Heintzelman, 2020.
Subjects: Romance | Humorous fiction| Holiday romance.

To Mommy
Thank you for cheering me on and reading everything I write

Airports are so weird. *Especially*, during the holidays. You start out in the terminal hefting around too many bags to fit the length of your trip. You're tired and anxious to get into a car and then on the road. As you make your way to passenger pickup, some rendition of "I'll Be Home for Christmas" is playing overhead. Instantly, you're nostalgic as your path is littered with Christmas trees and gigantic wreaths shoved between slot machines. Then, you step out to into the parking structure and it's *The Shining.*

Breathe, Bianca.

The sun is already low in the sky, making it feel darker and colder. My ears tune in to every voice and tire screech on the upper levels.

The automatic doors behind me swish open with a whoosh of cool air, giving me a start. When a pilot dragging his suitcase walks out, I try to settle my nerves, but my pulse is thumping. He dips his head in a small nod as he crosses the economy bus pickup on his way to employee parking.

And I'm alone down here again.

My heart is beating a mile a minute, but I guess this is what I get for letting my manager, Damien, plan "inconspicuous" transportation. *This is definitely low-key, Dame...and creepy.* I'm standing curbside on the dark commercial level at arrivals waiting for lord knows who, when a candy-apple-red sedan pulls up in front of me. I tighten my grip on the key wedged between my ring and middle fingers.

The driver lowers the window. I take a deep breath and lean down to look inside.

A slim, clean-cut, nerdy white dude with a Dexter haircut is at the wheel. He's in his mid-thirties. Just the type to get away with some *Bone Collector* taxi abduction shit in a sketchy-looking part of the airport.

His thin eyebrows slowly crease as he does a double take. "Rideo for Zoey?" he calls out to me in a questioning tone.

Immediately, I heave a sigh of relief, letting the knots in my stomach unravel. "That's me," I say, bending down to gather my tote and backpack.

Technically, it's not me, but you can't just broadcast on an app, "World-famous pop star, Bianca." It would be mayhem. Anyway, to avoid certain doom, Damien always gives me a celebrity name based on whichever TV show or movie he's obsessed with at the moment. I should've known after he binged three seasons of *New Girl* last night, it'd be a toss-up between the character Jess or the actress Zoey.

Strangely, I *could* break out into a random song right now. Though, it probably wouldn't have quite the festive ring to it considering I'm just happy to be alive right now.

"Zoey? Did I say that right?" the driver asks, still staring.

His eyes drift over me. He clearly knows who I am. The baseball cap, leggings, sweater, and boots I'm sporting—all black—are standard uniform for dodging paps at LAX. But

I'm not in La La Land anymore. This is McCarran airport. Vegas, baby—and all that entails—where you don't turn a blind eye, and you call a spade a spade.

"Let me—" He starts to get out of the car to get my suitcase, but I ward him off by holding my hand up in the air.

"I've got it." I shove my tote and purse into his spotless backseat. "Happy holidays. Thanks for picking me up. I can't wait to settle in. I'm exhausted," I say, tossing him a tiny smile meant to put a cork into the small talk.

He just ogles unblinking at me with his big brown eyes while I fumble with my giant suitcase. The man obviously recognizes me, but lucky for me, he seems intent on playing it cool—if only for a great rating and a tip worthy of a recording artist whose Christmas single is at the top of the charts for the fifth week in a row. *Woot! Woot!*

When I'm settled in the back with an audible harumph, he fires up his sensible hybrid electro-engine. At some point, he mumbles his name, but I'm not really listening because I'm too busy watching the road to make sure he's going in the right direction.

Dammit, the creepy parking structure is rubbing off on me.

Either way, I kind of like referring to him as the "Bone Collector." I'm sort of a stickler for not making people say their names twice.

B.C. weaves out of the terminal and onto the freeway, fiddling with the music once he's merged onto the 15. I'd like to say I'm surprised when he selects my song, "Mistletoe Memories," but I'm not. Everywhere I go, it's playing on repeat.

"You know, she's going to be playing at T-Mobile Arena at the Snowball Jam Christmas Day," he says, as if I tapped his seat and asked, "Hey, who is this singing?" Hints of a Midwestern accent rumble around between his words.

I'm curious, but I don't ask because he's still watching me, daring me to admit I'm Bianca and not Zoey. It's like a weird test, and he's committed to dying on this hill, which is just creepy.

Let it go, guy. Let it go.

Every few seconds, B.C.'s gaze flits to the rearview mirror and lands on me like he's checking to see if I'll sing along or outright state my identity. Forget the whole famous pop star bit. As far as he should be concerned, I'm just another fare using a rideshare app to get home safe for the holidays. He should keep his eyes on the road ahead.

As if on cue, my phone pings, saving me from a fatal rearview mirror staring contest. I hunch forward and fish it out of my back pocket.

Low and behold, it's Damien. *No surprise there.*

Damien 5:28 pm

Rest your voice and keep a low profile. I'm working on THE gig that's going to take your career to the next level.

I try not to put too much weight in Damien's words. If it's what I think it is, I don't want to get my hopes up. Tugging at my cap, I peek up. Again, B.C.'s gaze flickers up to the mirror, so I dip my chin.

Bianca 5:29pm

I haven't been home in five years. Unless Museik calls to offer me the tour, do refrain from calling me, please.

New Girl

Lol. I'll see you at the Snowball Jam in two weeks.

As much as seeing Mom and the house will inevitably bring the heavy memories flooding back, I just need to get away and not think about my next album or my career or where it's going next. I just need family and…hot chocolate with extra whipped cream.

And sprinkles.

A little less than half an hour later, I incline my head to discover, thankfully, my final destination is not a deserted building but the cute, single-story house with about a million string lights and a huge blow-up snowman on the lawn. It's the house where I grew up—*and left as soon as I got my first recording contract.*

The weight of being back here after so long away, settles in the pit of my stomach. *You can do this.* I take deep breaths, peering over to the house again.

I'm sure Mom is waiting by the door, so I scramble to get all of my bags out. Then B.C. wedges his body between the two front seats.

He looks at me with expectant eyes as I step out to the curb. His pensive expression catches me off guard. The defined lines of his face harden like he's weighing what to say.

Curiosity twists inside me.

The unobstructed, head-on view of him paints him in a different light—a much brighter, less creepy one. He could still be a good-looking serial killer who now knows where I'm staying, but there's a softness to him. He looks a little concerned and a tad bit bashful.

Because I'm such a headcase, I am naturally drawn to it.

"Yeah?" I prompt, urging him to say it.

His lips part, and his breaths are shallow. The whole delicious sheepish look is about as contagious as watching someone about to sneeze. I lean in, breathless to hear what he's got to say.

"I…" He swallows, and there's a slight shift in his shoulders like he's considering his next words. Then, he releases a breath and drops his chin. "Nothing, I...I was just going to say, if you need another ride, you can favorite me in the app...if, you're going to be around."

For a split second, I'm ransacking my mind trying to figure out what he was going to say before he decided not to. Suddenly, I can't tear my gaze away from his pouty lips.

Oh, my God, why am I staring so hard?

"Yeah, okay. Thanks."

He's cute in an adorable, nerdy sort of way, but he's my Rideo driver.

When I close this door, I'll likely never see him again. Which is just as well. I'm only here a couple of weeks, during which I plan to hide out with Mom and pack in as much holiday fun as we can before I'm hopefully off on a world tour. *It's for the best.* I'm guessing a hookup with Bone Collector on holiday isn't what Damien meant by "lay low."

So, I pat the roof of his car and lean down. Despite his sweeping dark lashes and a decidedly strong chin, I tell myself it's just my dusty lady parts having a nostalgic knee-jerk reaction to a cute guy.

Before I do anything stupid, I toss him a small smile. "Thanks again, and happy holidays." Then, I close his back door.

I don't even look back until he turns the corner.

***

"Stupid. So *stupid*."

Why didn't I just ask for her number? Maybe we could've had drinks. I could have tried a little more conversation to see what she had planned for the night. I groan.

How many times have I heard about rideshare drivers flirting with passengers and cringed in disgust?

Ah, it's not like I'm free tonight, anyway.

I blow out a breath, shaking my head as I hook a right at the corner headed for the freeway. It's Wednesday. My cousin Denise is probably two cocktails in already at Shane's, the off-Strip bar where she gets loaded on a weekly basis. She's a casino cocktail waitress Friday through Tuesday, so this is her weekend. Lucky me, I get to be her on-call chauffer to make sure she makes it home safe.

In the Brooks family, not showing up isn't an option.

When I make it to the freeway entrance, of course, the westbound lane is still bumper to bumper with the rush hour traffic. *Side roads it is.*

A few minutes later, when Denise's name lights up on the dashboard, I answer on Bluetooth. The cabin of the car fills with muffled background noise— mix of music and chatter.

"Hey. I should be there in like twenty."

"Don't rush. Lena's here." Denise slurs. *Probably two whiskey sours by now.* "It's jam-packed tonight."

"All right. You hungry?" I ask, hoping to help her soak up some of the alcohol. The last thing I need is an accident in here. I just got my car detailed. "It's no big deal. I can grab you a quick bite—"

"No, I'm good for now. Just come hang out with us. Take a load off for *once*. The band is so *intense*. They're doing Christmas favorites."

I chuckle, trying to reconcile the image in my head of a hardcore grunge band singing cheery holiday songs. Then my mind drags me back to Zoey and how stupid I must've sounded using the Snowball Jam to drum up conversation. The commercial plays every hour on the hour.

A blaring horn startles me as a black truck speeds past.

"Yeah, all right... Okay, I'll be there soon."

For a few seconds, I think Denise hung up on me, but her name is still on the dash and the muffled music from the bar is still playing. "D?"

"Jaden, what's wrong with you?" she asks. "What happened? Why are you so distracted?" I can already imagine the alcohol-fueled wheels in her head spinning out.

"Hmm?"

"You're just going to have drinks with us without me begging? Obviously, something's going on."

My shoulders tense, and my pulse revs. Denise is like a fun-sized bloodhound with her goth black hair, bold red lipstick, and unmatched bullshit radar. She knows how to sniff out the slightest change in the air.

Better to tell her now, rather than in a bar full of people.

"It's nothing, really. You know how it is. All night it's been dead, right? Then, *ping*, an airport pickup." I slap the steering wheel. "Figured I had time before rescuing you, to make a little cash. Except, she was—"

"I knew it. You're totally crushing on your passenger!" Denise squeals, cutting right to the chase. "Was she interested?"

The light up ahead turns yellow, and I slow to a stop.

"That's the thing. There might have been *something* there... I just didn't feel right asking for her number. That feels like crossing the line. Doesn't it seem sleazy to you, flirting with a passenger?"

Denise ignores everything I just said. "Let me guess...a typical Vegas club girl with the plastic boobs and lips?"

"No." I release a short bark of laughter. "When has that ever been my type? This girl was nothing like that at all. I mean, she was at the airport, so she was dressed for travel. Maybe Latina...average height...not too skinny, but fit...

curly hair in a ponytail and light makeup… It was more than looks, though. There was something more in her eyes. She seemed warm…genuine."

When Denise doesn't say anything, I listen to the muffled bar sounds.

In classic Denise form, she brings our conversation to a halt to recap my dilemma to her friend. I hear every word, though—their sarcastic tones while they debate my "textbook party foul," how I'm too much of a "decent" guy to take any risks.

My blood boils a little because maybe I would be more carefree if I wasn't always looking out for others and for family. Maybe if I wasn't worried about some trash dude slipping her a rufie and having his way with her, I might be out with friends on a weekday, or joining a beautiful woman in my backseat instead of staring at her like "decent" guys do.

As I pull into the small parking lot on the side of Shane's, Denise and Lena are still in my ear debating the merits of good guys versus hot bad boys. They've forgotten I'm here.

"Denise?" My tone is sharp.

There's rustling as she comes back. "Oh, shit. I'm sorry—"

I abruptly press the button to disconnect. It doesn't have the same effect as slamming a phone down and letting the dial tone echo in her ear, but I end the call feeling vindicated.

The way I see it, the score is: shit-faced cousin, zero, "decent guy," one.

CHAPTER TWO

Before I reach the red, belted "Santa door," Mom swings it open and pulls me into a hug. I'm wrapped up in her warm, sugar cookie scent, her soft skin, and the easiness of her breathing.

"Thank God you made it." She falls into old habits, petting my hair like she's always done. I've missed her doing it more than I allow myself to admit.

"Hey there, pretty lady," I murmur into her soft dark curls, absorbing the comforting feel of her.

I send her tickets to come out to L.A. all the time, but there's something so nostalgic and easy—melancholy—about seeing her in *this* doorframe. Mom alone always reminds me that Dad will never be standing there with her.

"Oof, you know I don't trust those Rideo drivers," she comments, worried about me as usual. "It's not safe for young women. What if he decided to take you to some remote building—"

"Mom..." The whine that slips through my lips, melts into a laugh.

This is why my mind spirals the way it does.

When she releases me, we gather my luggage together and enter the house—*my* house with the warm fireplace where Dad and I read *Goosebumps* together, the kitchen where we made Sunday brunch, and the hallway lined with family photos. With a heavy heart, I step all the way inside, but I don't have time to linger on all the Christmas decorations or family keepsakes.

I'm struck by the sight of Margo's long blonde hair and even longer legs hooked over the arms. Cara is nestled in the crook of her knees. My heart leaps out of my chest, and I drop my bags with a shriek.

"What are you guys doing here?"

My best and lifelong friends are sprawled out on…wait, that's not Daddy's favorite lumpy couch. A new, sleek navy-blue sofa sits where it once was. I don't even have a chance to process the new furniture.

When they see me, they abandon the holiday movie playing on Flixshow, jolt upright, and lunge for me. Cara's textured curls and Margo's big boobs are in my face. There's lots of hugging and prodding as they call dibs on my accessories and clothes. I notice they are not dressed in anything close to "Relax and Flixshow" attire.

I survey their skyscraper heels and bandage dresses. "Um, where are you going tonight?"

Margo clears her throat. With a flutter of her sweeping eyelashes, she corrects me. "Where are *'we'* going?" She emphasizes.

"Ladies Night at Shane's!" Cara sings the words as she does a little shimmy dance. "I'm hoping this band I love plays tonight, but either way, free drinks and cute guys with my girls. We are single and ready to mingle."

I flit a tentative glance over my shoulder at Mom who

doesn't seem irritated in the least that I literally just walked through the door after being gone for years, and already my friends are dragging me out.

She waves me off. "Go on. Have a good time." She presses a velvety hand to her red and white polka dot sweater. *Is that new?* "Makes me feel so good to see you girls back together again. It's been too long, Bianca."

Margo and Cara shoot me pointed stares, clearly in agreement with Mom.

Five years *is* way too long. My heart plummets to my stomach just thinking of how much I've missed all these years away. Even if they have visited me, why haven't I come back more?

My heart wrenches.

"Well, I'm here for two weeks." I clap my hands, shaking off the weight of my thoughts. "Let's make the most of it, and pack every day with something fun and Christmas-y. I want to bake, make cards, craft...throw some ugly sweater parties. You name it, I'm in. And maybe..." I tilt my head with a smile. "You all will come hang out with me at the Snowball Jam."

The high-pitched shrieks from my friends spur another group hug.

When they release me this time, I'm actually kind of excited about getting out for a night in my hometown. It'll be a chance to make up for lost time.

"Okay. Let's do this. Should I change, throw on some heels? I brought a few hats and wigs." I waggle my eyebrows. "In case we need to keep things low key."

"Nope, it's going to be so packed." Cara stares at her reflection in a glass ornament and reapplies her bright red lipstick. "No one is going to be paying you any attention."

Once I've slipped out of my sweater and into a cute, silky

blouse and heels to go with my jeans, we kiss Mom, and we're off.

The lot at Shane's is full, so we have to park a block down on the street. I don't mind the cold, though. The light chill is just enough to enjoy the season.

The rush of heat and music when we open the door leaves me feeling right at home. Almost immediately, I notice two things. First, Cara was right. It is packed. No one has given me a second glance. Second, Shane's has changed.

A lot.

It used to have an English pub feel—a bit dim, but still cheery. Now it's dark and moody with low lights. Lots of black, brick, and galvanized metals fuse into a natural palette with a sleek, industrial edge. It's modern, but also stark and eclectic in a cool way—almost like it's grown up, too.

We weave our way through a sea of people, blending in, as we reach a small opening.

"Oh. My. Gosh," Margo stops in her tracks, and her marble green eyes widen.

I follow her line of vision to the stage on the far back wall where three bearded guys and a bombshell of woman command the crowd. Their boho, grungy vibe and the bluesy rock mix is different than anything I've heard, especially, in a holiday song.

How do they make "The Christmas Song" sound so sexy?

"They're here." Cara announces. Even in heels so tall my feet hurt just looking at them, she's on her tiptoes angling to get a better look. "These guys were here a couple of months ago and they are *insanely* good. They ended up getting in a huge fight with someone in the crowd, so we figured they wouldn't be back, but, oh…they are amazing."

"Yeah?" I nod, surveying them again with a new interest.

They sound great, but I also know Cara is a sucker for men with beards.

Still, this place and the atmosphere is what I miss being in the music industry. I don't miss bar fights or handsy fans. I miss the grass-roots connection with the people and the freedom when it's not about your last record or which charts you've topped. I miss playing just because it feels good for the soul.

I flit another glance at the band over my shoulder then lower my chin, letting my hair fall into my face.

"Let's gets some drinks then," I say, clinging to Margo's arm.

We move with the current as the song changes. The beat picks up with a soulful rendition of "Merry Christmas, Happy Holidays." The three of us move to the rhythm of the crowd. We're swaying our hips and bobbing our heads as we beeline for the long, black, lacquered bar on the left side of the room.

As soon as I slide onto a stool, the day catches up with me. I throw my head back and crack my neck, letting the tension drain from my shoulders. Usually, I like to wash the flight off and get comfy the first night I travel.

I'm only here for two weeks.

A couple of minutes later, the bartender slides six shots in front of us. They're a dark brown color with a thick texture I haven't seen before.

I flash the girls a questioning look.

They don't even blink.

"Drink up," Margo says as she tosses back her first one. She scrunches up her face, which should be the first sign not to follow suit, then she dips her shoulder to mine. "Hot chocolate shots…whipped cream, vodka…"

Say no more.

If there are two things I love about the holidays, it's hot chocolate—even if it's cold and spiked—and whipped cream. Tipping my head back, I swallow my first one. I come up for air feeling like I can literally breathe fire.

"Yes! It's like Christmas in a fun-sized dose." I chuckle.

Margo and Cara waste no time with theirs, so they're already off their stools with their bodies angled toward the dance floor.

"Okay. All right." Pouting, I lift my teensy glass to the saint of hangovers and mornings after. Then I set it to my lips.

I drain the entire shot into my mouth, then I start to shimmy off the stool, and... *What in the actual hell?*

Margo and Cara must see my shock because they curve their bodies out of the way just in time as I do a spit take. Teensy brown droplets go flying past them to the floor and...onto B.C.

Is he actually a stalker who followed me here?

My mouth refuses to close. My motor skills are apparently defunct. I cannot move despite the urge to lunge forward.

"Seriously, B?" Cara's still shaking her head when she turns around.

My stalker Rideo driver is drenched in my hot chocolate shot. *That'll teach you to follow women around.*

Margo, never the one to catch on right away, actually purrs whilst ogling him. "Ooh. He is *cute.*" But as her gaze travels down his sculpted chest, she eventually cringes for me. "And pissed."

"I'm the one who should be mad. He's the freaking *Bone Collector,*" I scoff, and three pairs of eyes snap to mine. "Don't tell me you didn't see that movie with Angelina Jolie and Denzel Washington where the serial killer cab driver locks them in the car?"

His thick brows shoot up. Amusement flickers across his face.

Yeah, you saw the movie.

Ever the relentless flirt, Margo ignores me and grabs a stack of napkins from the bar. Marching right up to him, she dabs at his pecks and biceps, missing all the brown stains on his white Henley. The woman is practically salivating as she feels him up.

I cross my arms, feeling my expression pinch

"He was my Rideo driver," I interject, hoping to insert some reason into this quickly escalating situation.

Cara shrugs, failing to follow my logic.

"Clearly, he's following me." I narrow my gaze at him. "Did you follow me here? Are you stalking me?"

A flash of anger shoots through me and I have no clue if it really is about him following me. This is a public bar. I'm the one who just spewed my drink on him. *He* should be mad.

Well, he certainly looks pissed.

His gaze flicks upward and he clenches his jaw as he plucks the wet fabric from his impressive abs.

"Wow. I didn't know you were the only one allowed in this *public* bar," he says. "Should I notify everyone else your permission is required to be here?"

Asshole…. Hot asshole.

It could be the dim light in the bar, but the sharp contrasting lines of his strong jaw almost look sinister—in the hottest sense. Honestly, his bone structure isn't the only thing I notice. His expressive warm brown eyes from the driver's seat earlier are now cold and dark as he glares at me from beneath his sweeping lashes.

I never got a full look at him—just small doses from the curb, in the rearview mirror, or looking down into the car at him. But up close, inches apart...

B.C. is tall. He' not basketball player tall, but tall enough to easily reach the top kitchen cupboard. He's got lean muscles, neatly tapered dark hair, and a deliciously sweet mouth.

Shit.

"I think I should." He throws his hands up, scanning the crowd with that stupid adorable smirk on his face. "Matter of fact, I'll go tell the manager he only has *one* person who deserves to be here tonight. Everyone else should immediately leave the premises."

When the band announces they're going a fifteen-minute break, he lifts his chin dramatically like there'll be an announcement any minute.

"Whatever. You can try to play it off. I already know."

A smile plays on B.C.'s lips as the music changes to a low buzz above the chatter.

"I'm still waiting for my apology." He pinches his shirt fabric off his skin drawing my eyes to his abs.

Margo and Cara haven't said a word. They seem fully entertained by this little "disagreement" between their best friend and her hot stalker Rideo driver. Their eyes keep darting back and forth between us like it's a dang tennis match.

I don't care how cute he is. I've dealt with this type of thing too many times to count. I have to confront them.

"Oh. You think you deserve an apology?" *Fat chance.* "Let me get this straight, first you're my Rideo driver and now you show up at the same random, off-strip bar an hour later...*by chance?*" I cock my head and give a half shrug before folding my arms over my chest.

He throws his hands up with a laugh. "You're crazy. Maybe you should learn how to handle your liquor."

My blood boils, and any humor or attraction I might have had to this guy is gone. "Admit it. You know who I am," I demand.

"Look, I hate to disappoint you, but..." His eyes drift from my head to my toes before he lifts them and pins me with a heated stare. His tongue dips out to lick his lips, and my stomach clenches. "You're not the only star in *my* galaxy, sweetheart."

My mouth falls open.

I knew it.

Erasing the distance between us, I'm right up in his face. "Yeah, okay buddy. Is that why you told me to favorite you on the app?" I scoff. My tone is sharp, dripping with sarcasm. I dare him to deny he followed me.

Triple-dog dare him.

Before I can up my ante, a woman ducks beneath B.C.'s arm, inserting herself into the mix. She's short and curvy but fit with long, straight black hair. She's strikingly beautiful and probably throws back two holiday shots with no problem.

I sink my fingers into my scalp, lifting my own windblown waves.

"Thought you were bringing us beers," the woman says with a little slur, swaying forward. She loses her footing, and as B.C. catches her, the weight of her slate gray eyes hits me like a wrecking ball.

She blinks, and I know that wide-eyed look.

Right at the lull in the song, she sucks in a breath and shouts, "Holy shit. It's Bianca!"

Dammit, I should've worn a hat.

AND I'M JADEN.

I glance at Denise and shrug as she rights herself on her sky-high heels. She's still staring, slack-jawed at the woman who—if I recall the name from the app—is named Zoey, not Bianca.

"Okay, D. Maybe we should call it," I say.

My immediate reaction is to correct Denise and cut her off for the rest of the night. She only gets water for the next half hour before I take the chance of putting her in my freshly detailed backseat. But then I notice the wide-eyed, surprised look on her face.

She hasn't snapped out of it. Her posture is awkwardly rigid, and she still looks disoriented.

"D? What's going on here?" I ask again.

The woman, Zoey or Bianca, fixes her gaze on Denise. It's like she's waiting to see what my cousin's next move will be. None of us have moved, but then an important detail occurs to me. Denise called this woman by a different name, but she didn't correct her.

"So, how do you two know each other?" I flit a glance between them.

My question seems to startle the woman.

"She's—" Denise cuts herself off as the woman shoots her a pleading stare. Her expression wars between fear and desperation as she gives a small, panicked head shake.

Then her gaze shifts to me.

For a beat I hold her stare, not quite sure what's happening. Then something over my shoulder snags her attention. Her eyes slowly scan the room, and her forehead creases as she turns. Then, as if they're connected, both of her friends do the same.

"Should we, maybe take this outside?" I ask tentatively.

Apparently, our little commotion has gained the attention of a few dozen more pairs of eyes. And they're pointing their phones at this...Bianca.

What's the plan here, J?

"Uh, I'm sorry about your shirt." Her voice is shaky as she steps backward.

The carefree friend with the long blonde hair who'd patted me down earlier, eyes the door. "We have to go. *Now*," she says with conviction.

As soon as they turn away, a group of people move with them, rushing toward them.

"Am I missing something? What exactly is happening?" I ask.

Denise's eyes are still fixed on the door. "That was Bianca. As in number-one-song-on-the-charts-right-now Bianca. Sold-out-Snowball-Jam Bianca."

I lift my chin, and my shoulders tense. A light tingling sweeps over the back of my neck and cheeks. "Oh."

Now Denise looks at me. "*Oh?* You were talking to a certified pop star, and all you have to say is '*oh?*' You're acting so weird tonight."

My eyes snap to the door now, too.

Not that her celebrity status changes anything, but it explains a whole lot. When I think back to the drive from the airport and how she'd searched the car, and me, before entering... How stupid I must've sounded telling her about her own song *and sold out concert*. I groan and jam my hands in my pockets. I actually told her to favorite me on the app. *Idiot!*

"The airport pickup from earlier...the woman who I thought there 'might've been something' with?" I pause, taking it in myself. "That was her."

Denise blinks slowly and steps directly in front of me. "Your Rideo pickup was Bianca?"

"Apparently."

She clutches my shoulders and lowers her chin. She must have a million questions in her head.

How is it that everyone in the world knows who this woman is except for me?

I can practically see smoke coming out of D's ears.

"And now all these people know it's her...because of me." She closes her eyes, shaking her head. "We have to do something."

"Like what? If she's a celebrity pop star like you say, I'm sure she's used to this sort of thing."

"And what if something happens to them? They're leaving a bar. I'm sure they've been *drinking*," she says, dragging the last word out as she pops her head up. Her eyes are round and full of what I can already tell is a really bad idea. "*Unlike* a certain *decent guy* I know, who'd never let a beautiful starlet or her friends drink and drive, thus putting innocent lives in danger, or her career, at risk."

Ah, the guilt trip...

I throw my head back and scrub my hands over my face. "Why do you do this to me?" I groan.

"That's why everyone loves you. You always do the right thing." Denise bats her eyes. "Come on. You know you want to see her again. All we have to do is to go out and make sure they're okay and that they didn't get mobbed by crazy fans or paparazzi. Did you see any bodyguards?"

When I lower my chin, Denise pouts.

As I blow out an exasperated sigh, she adds, "We'll just drive around the block once or twice. If they're gone, we've done our good deed for the night."

Simple as that.

Funny, though. Everything about it screams "complicated."

CHAPTER THREE

"Bianca! Take a selfie with me!" A guy shouts.

"Will you sign this?" Another girl asks, holding out a crumpled store receipt she fishes out from her tote.

Outside Shane's, my girls and I are surrounded on all sides by a mob of half-drunk, half-manic people. Most are from the bar. But a few people who happened to be walking and driving by when we spilled out onto the street have joined them.

"Sure." I flash a tight smile to no one in particular.

There are a few dozen cameras aimed at me, waiting for me to do something post-worthy. I should be thinking about my safety without a bodyguard, but all I can think about is how much fun it was bickering with B.C. and how adorably boyish he looked when I apologized about his shirt.

I swallow and dig out a Sharpie from my purse.

Along with a Wally World receipt, I sign T-shirts, caps, arms, and even a guy's harry chest with a smile pasted on. It's not that I mind smiling for a few pictures and chatting up a small group of fans. They're my community. They buy my records and follow me on social media. I genuinely love and appreciate my fans. They're the reason that Damien will hopefully call to tell me Museik wants me on the tour.

The problem is, a selfie or an autograph is never enough.

And this small group isn't so small anymore. There's shouting, waving hands, and people pushing into each other to get to me. I feel my pulse quicken and my stomach harden.

"We love you, Bianca."

"'Mistletoe Memories' is my mom's favorite Christmas song."

Margo and Cara lock arms and burrow through a small opening in the pack while dragging me close behind. Cara's already got her phone out calling for a Rideo since we've been drinking.

"It's fine. I'll sign a couple more." I give a small shrug flashing a smile at a girl behind a curtain of red curls. She's all heart and genuine admiration, and she seems so out of place here. I take her phone and hand it to Cara, huddling close for one more photo.

"On three say, 'hard candy Christmas.'"

The girl laughs, and we both beam at the phone.

"One. Two..."

Angling the phone, on the screen I notice the smiling faces around me beginning to twist to creased foreheads and gaping mouths. It's a tell-tale panicked flush when they don't know how to come down from the high of seeing a celebrity in person. My pulse quickens, and my heartbeat picks up.

"Three."

I tilt my head and lift my chin, ready to get this photo op

over with, when a movement behind Cara snares my attention.

Bone Collector.

And the woman who said my name.

She's latched onto his arm as the wind whips through her long black hair. Her hot pink lipstick is smudged …

Cara snaps a few more shots and quickly hands the girl back her phone. She whispers through a closed-tooth smile. "B, let's go."

My throat tightens as I turn to the girl, catching a glimpse of B.C. in my peripheral. "All right. You guys take care."

The crowd immediately grows antsy, following us as we walk away. They match our pace until we reach the corner, but as Margo takes off, pulling me with her, the people start running after us.

Just a few more pictures.

A couple more autographs.

"We really do have to get going. But thank you all so much and happy holidays," I yell back to them, waving. "I hope you'll all check me out at the Snowball Jam on Christmas!"

"Holy shit!" Cara screams, her wild curls bouncing as she sprints in five-inch heels.

Being chased by a mob of fans is always sobering, but we've just taken two holiday hot chocolate shots. By the way my vision blurs and my legs wobble, I'm pretty sure they were like 100 proof.

Where is the Rideo?

Margo, whose feet are way more comfortable in heels than athletic shoes, takes the lead, running up ahead. She tosses a glance over her shoulder. "We have to make it to the car."

Through the haze, I manage to pick up my pace.

As we come up on the next corner, a familiar candy apple red sedan swerves in front of us like something out of an action movie.

"Get in!" Bone Collector yells.

I really need to ask this guy for his name.

Margo and Cara don't even hesitate. They hop in the backseat with his... Is she his *girlfriend*? There's no time to stop and contemplate what kind of dude would put his whatever she is to him in the backseat.

Scrambling to open the passenger door, I jump into the front and breathe a relieved sigh as he banks a left, leaving the mob in his dust.

"So," I say, clicking my seatbelt.

B.C. glances over at me, his brows dipped in concern. "You all right, there, Zoey?"

He flashes me a cocky, half-grin before returning his attention to the road.

Considering how this night is shaping up, I just might favorite him.

"Where to, ladies?" I turn the radio volume down and flick on my indicator. "I can pull up the address from earlier if you need me to."

Before Bianca can answer, the blonde leans forward, wedging herself between our seats. "Nope. It's your first night back in town. You're not going home yet."

Behind us, her curly-headed friend and Denise hum their agreement. They're antsy and hyped up from the getaway. Honestly, so am I. Although, I think my nerves have more to do with the beautiful woman sitting beside me.

The vibe I got from her as she got out of my car when I

dropped her off is back. It's like a live wire between us with sparks and heat. I feel like if we touched, it would be explosive.

"Ooh, downtown." Curly moans as she slouches in the middle of the backseat. "They've turned Fremont Street into Winter Wonderland. It's like a neon Christmas on steroids. Snow, caroling, crafts for the kids, everything."

Denise whistles. "I'm all about sitting on Santa's lap right now."

A chorus of drunk giggles echoes from the backseat.

"What about O'Sullivan's?" Curly adds, making her case for a downtown destination, but then she adds, "Irish men are so freaking *hot*." She practically moans the last word.

The three of them go on like this, falling into the comfort of mindless conversation. They discuss the merits of beards and accents. Oh, and my all-time favorite, the "off-the-charts" hotness factor of men with red hair and piercing blue-green eyes.

I'm the odd man out on all fronts.

Bianca flits a sheepish glance at me, cringing as they begin to list examples. After Colin Farrell and Jonathan Rhys Meyers, I officially tune out.

"Sorry. My friends have no filters." Bianca shrugs, but the smile quirking her full lips steals my breath.

Just looking at her, I know my cousin is wrong about me. I'm a decent guy when it comes to morals and ethics. Sure, I look out for Denise once a week when her shifts at the casino take the worst toll on her. But when Bianca levels me with a pleading stare, I'm bad. Images of me pressing her up against a wall and kissing her until she's breathless and moaning overtake everything good in me.

Don't get ahead of yourself.

Heat coats my skin, crawling from my neck to my cheeks.

I tug at my collar and force a smile. "Three drunks and us, Zoey," I tease. Denise already told me who she is, but I want it to be her who lets me in.

We laugh as I change lanes to merge onto the freeway.

"Actually, it's Bianca," she says, surprising me.

I nod, my lower lip protruding as the corners of my mouth tug downward. "Ah. So not Zoey?"

After a beat, she peeks over her shoulder at Denise. When she sits back, her anxious face and stiff posture give her away.

Through the rearview mirror, Denise widens her eyes and tips her head forward, giving me the little push I need.

I adjust my legs, slouching for more leg room. "Bianca suits you better than Zoey."

She takes a minute to explain her code names for anonymity, but I'm waiting for her to tell me the rest. I want her full story and anything else she's willing to share with me. I want to know her, not the celebrity.

"Should we do introductions, then? This is the second time I'm seeing you in as many hours. Also, it might be nice not to be referred to as 'Bone Collector.'" I chuckle, remembering what she'd called me back at Shane's.

Bianca covers her face with her hands and laughs.

"You have to admit, the way you pulled up all creepy down on that dark commercial level...I was freaked out. And I didn't hear your name when you said it, so I've been calling you B.C."

"Wow. If I'm not mistaken, we're coming up on Christmas. Don't tell me you're one of those people stuck on Halloween..."

I veer toward the exit and turn off the freeway onto Casino Center, looking left as I ease onto the one-way street.

When I peek back at Bianca, she's still alight with amusement.

"Maybe." She twists in the seat to face me, waving off the comment. "Back to your original question. If you want to be formal about this, I'm Bianca…Esposito, if you want a legal name. The two crazy ones back there, they've been my best friends since middle school."

"Nice."

"Margo is the tall blonde who enjoyed cleaning my shot off of you—a little too much, I think." She tilts her head to the side to toss her friend a silly face. "Sorry about that, by the way. The fun-sized one with the big smile and fabulous curls is Cara."

Cara makes a whooping noise to confirm her presence before going back to their surprisingly extensive discussion on the physical features of Irish men. It's good to have everyone's actual names now. I decide to return the favor.

"That's my cousin, Denise." I jerk my thumb over my shoulder, catching the tail-end of a smile on Bianca's lips. "I'm Jaden…Brooks, if you need my last name to scratch me off the serial killer list." I draw my finger across my throat with a laugh.

On the radio, "Jingle Bell Rock" is playing on the lowest volume.

I pause for a beat, weighing my question. "So, are you really this pop star my cousin keeps telling me about?"

She nods, her eyes darting to the dashboard like she gets my correlation between her and the music. She rakes her fingers through her hair as she turns to the window with a faraway look on her face. Her shoulders sag a little. I'm starting to like Bianca with her guard down.

"You must've thought I was an idiot telling you about Snowball Jam and your own song."

Bianca surveys me for a brief moment before a smile toys with her lips. "I have to admit, it's weirdly refreshing that you didn't know who I was." She giggles, scrunching her nose in embarrassment. "I thought you were just playing it cool and failing miserably. Although, it does sort of make me the asshole for accusing you of stalking me." She drops her face into her palm.

I tap my finger to my nose, playfully indicating she's on the right track.

She flips her hand, palm up then down. "It was pretty cute."

"It was." I admit.

We both laugh now.

Slowing with the traffic, I lean against the headrest. "So, you've just gotten into town? Where are you from?" I ask with a quick glance.

"I'm from here, actually. It's just been a while since I visited, but I'm here until the day after Christmas."

I nod. "Making up for lost time?"

Her whole face lights up. "Exactly. I might be going on tour soon. For now, I just want two weeks of festive, holiday fun—no plans or itineraries." She breathes a sigh, closing her eyes.

I lift an eyebrow and blow out my cheeks. "Phew. Sounds like you're ready to take on the town. I don't know if Santa's ready…"

"You'll laugh," Bianca whips her gaze back to me and holds up her finger. "I was just telling the girls how I want to pack the days with everything Christmas. This night definitely qualifies, don't you think? I just want to do something for me without thinking of my career or if I'll be on tour in a couple of weeks. I want to do something…" Her tone has an air of whimsy and lightness as she trails off. "Spontaneous."

Even before she says the word, I know what she means. For a while now, the urge to do something out of character has been nagging at me. I don't want to think about the fragility of life and how the ones I love could be here today and gone tomorrow. Adventure is what I need.

Spontaneity.

I give her a mock salute. "It will be my sole mission tonight."

"Jaden, you are so lame," Denise groans. "At least buy the woman a drink if you're going to talk her ear off." She turns to Bianca. "You'll have to excuse my cousin. He lives under a boring rock. It's hard to tell, but he's a decent guy."

Not a compliment, D.

Margo and Cara hum their approval of nice guys, but I don't miss how Bianca levels me with a stare. Wait... *Is that heat in her eyes?*

"What do you say? Let me buy you a drink," I suggest.

She drums her fingers on her thigh then shrugs. "It's Christmas. I'm hanging with three drunks and the Bone Collector. What isn't there to celebrate?"

O'SULLIVAN'S IS THE FLASHIEST IRISH BAR I'VE EVER SEEN. Keeping with the downtown Winter Wonderland theme, it's Christmas for Saint Paddy. There's beer to keep us jolly and servers going around wishing people the blessings of Christmas...in fake Irish accents.

There are neon green lights, shamrocks, snow, and a diminutive Santa in a green velvet suit. The best part is, they sell bright green wigs that are good enough to disguise a pop star on a night out with friends.

As it turns out, the car conversation between the three

drunks was only a prelude to their appreciation for Irish men. Of course, the tall, bearded, tattooed guys Denise, Margo, and Cara are sidled up to may not even be Irish. I scrutinize them for good measure.

"Should we..." Bianca's words die off as she flits a nervous glance over to the bar, and I follow her line of vision.

Cara erupts with laughter at something one of the guys said, throwing her head back. The stool wobbles, and she latches onto the guy's bicep for balance.

I chuckle. "Nah. They're just having a good time, but I'll keep an eye out."

Bianca and I hang at the other end of the bar. We're away from the music and the endless pairs of curious eyes wondering about the green-haired girl who's a doppel-gänger for that pop star with the Christmas song.

I've noticed the stares, but I'm still too busy trying to wrap my mind around the fact that I'm the lucky SOB who somehow landed her undivided attention. It's a few hours during one night in Vegas, so I don't read too much into it.

Bianca's still talking about the airport pickup as she twines our fingers together. But then she swipes her thumb over my palm. My dick twitches in response.

Fuck. I hate being the decent guy.

I flash her a soft smile and order a water for me and a hot chocolate shot for Bianca.

"No. I just...you looked so creepy," she says laughing.

"Noted. I'll have to remember to stay away from dark airport structures," I say, scraping a hand through my hair.

She tosses back her shot and scrunches her face. "Damn those things are so good. But no, it was the lights and the way you pulled up super slow and stared all serial killer-like..." She leans in too close like she might bump into me.

"Okay. You've made your point." I laugh.

"I had a sharp key between my fingers to shank you…" Her giggle fades.

Across the room, the song changes to a mellow groove and she starts to sway. I'm not sure if it's because of the melody or if she's at her limit for the night.

"You okay? Should we switch you to water, too?" I dip my head to examine her eyes and movements, but I'm so close, she could almost—

Bianca lightly brushes her lips over mine with a moan. Her hands are flat on my chest. Then she twists the fabric in her fists. She pulls away with a lazy smile on her soft, pillowy lips.

"You taste like chocolate and mint."

My whole body locks up. I don't know what I'm supposed to do here. Do I want to kiss her? Fuck yeah. While her judgment's impaired? Also, yes. But it just feels wrong.

"Maybe I should cut you off, too," I say trying to ignore the way my dick throbs.

My pulse quickens, and my mind races. She's a beautiful woman, a desirable *celebrity* whose picture probably inspires pre-teen fantasies. She's coming on to me. And I can't stop analyzing it long enough to appreciate how good she feels.

Get out of your head, Jaden.

"So, two weeks, huh?" I swallow hard, trying to keep my eyes north. I remind myself she's leaving. *But…* "My family's having an ugly sweater party on the nineteenth. Does that meet your Christmas adventure requirements?" I ask.

"You really are a decent guy, aren't you?"

God, I'm so fucking tired of that word.

Heat pools in her eyes as she slides her tongue over her lower lip. My heart knocks around in my chest.

Slowly, I lean forward, seeking and finding her lips. It's tender and sweet. *Like a fucking nice guy…*

As if she's privy to my internal spiral, she leans back to study me under hooded eyes. "Try again," she says between sweet kisses.

I'm not about to strike out and have this be the story I tell ten years from now. *I almost kissed Bianca once, but I couldn't get my shit together.* I'm holding back. Why am I holding back?

This could be the best one-night stand of my life.

"I like decent guys, Jaden, but I want them to kiss like dirty, bad boys." She purrs, adding fuel to my already out of control fire.

Fuck it.

Before I can overthink it, I cup her face between my hands and deepen the kiss. Dipping my tongue between her lips, I move in sweeping licks, exploring, tasting her moans. With my tongue, I tease hers. Our breaths come fast and shallow. Her hands clench in my shirt fabric, almost sending me over the edge.

When I erase the space between us, tugging her flush to me, I slip my hands beneath the hem of her thin shirt. The pads of my fingers blaze where our skin touches.

How's that for a decent guy?

This time when we pull apart, Bianca's eyes are still closed. She doesn't move. She just moans her approval.

That's right.

"Holy Christmas." She drags her eyes open and plops down on the barstool, pressing her hand to her chest. "Jaden." *My name on her tongue like that…* "It's the best of both worlds, you decent, dirty, dirty boy. Marry me?"

Those two words stick with me the rest of the night.

We dance ourselves silly and smile for another one of

Cara's "'tis the season" photos. We make our way out into the crux of the Winter Wonderland and throw snowballs at each other. She accidentally nails me in the face, then kisses it all better.

The way she makes me feel, I will be her playboy and her dirty boy. If it means this will last longer than just tonight, I'll do it. Right now, she isn't a famous pop star inching toward a wild one-night stand with a full-time accountant and part-time Rideo driver who spends his nights worried about his brother.

Tonight, she's the gorgeous woman who makes me feel like I have a life of my own to live—even if it is only for a few hours.

When we're all partied out, the five of us set out on the four-block trek to Denise's downtown apartment. The three drunks walk ahead. As we bring up the rear, the woman who made me feel alive is holding my hand. The moment we end up in front of the Gold Band Chapel, two words come rushing to the forefront of my mind like a spontaneous call to adventure.

CHAPTER FOUR

"Get. Up."

I roll over into a foot and crack my eyes open. By the bright red toenails glinting off the sun, it clearly belongs to Margo.

Hot chocolate shots and Irish beer... *Why?*

"What?" I groan against the pounding of my head, yanking the blanket over my eyes.

Margo yanks it down again. "Holy shit. Wake up." She bounces up and down, shaking the mattress, rousing Cara on her other side. With her free hand she slaps me on my ass. But her gaze is locked on her phone. "I'm famous."

You have got to be kidding me...

"Shh. I'm begging you, *please*. We all know you're fabulous and fierce, but people are trying to sleep here." I whine. The second the words escape my lips they die on my tongue.

People.

My eyelids snap open.

I take in the modern two-tone white and slate walls and

the floor-to-ceiling windows where I'd peered out at the panoramic city view of Las Vegas last night.

More people than me and my girls.

My heart stutters, and my throat tightens.

Slowly, I look past Cara. *Denise, the cousin.*

I take in a deep breath and turn over, and there he is. Curled at my side with his dark hair hanging in his face is my Rideo driver. Jaden Brooks: part-time getaway driver, full-time accountant, and all-around decent guy…*who kisses like sin.*

My breath catches in my throat. *We kissed…multiple times.*

And it was good. Better than good, it was mind-blowingly delicious. I wanted him…

I remember the feel of his full lips nipping mine, his tongue sweeping and exploring my mouth, and my pulse quickens. Absently, I press my fingers to my lips.

"You need to see this," Margo says, but I can't concentrate on her fame at the moment. I'm a bit busy trying to recount the blacked-out timeline of last night.

Did we… With other people in the bed?

Last night floods to the surface of my memory. The two of us started at O'Sullivan's. We'd laughed and danced, took pictures with St. Paddy Claus. A giggle bubbles up inside me. Cara with her dang phone, so many pictures of us screaming "'tis the season" at the top of our lungs, me in that crazy green wig…

The fog around the night slowly thins.

"Oh my God, B. Both the special edition wedding planner and my Crimson Queen lipstick. Completely sold out." Margo's scrolling on her phone, shaking her head like her newfound fame is such a shock.

"I told you it was only a matter of time. Your makeup

and accessories are like every diva planner's dream," I say, but I can't tear my eyes away from Jaden.

We'd spilled out into the Winter Wonderland. The Snowball fight, the never-ending walk to Denise's downtown apartment... We held hands nearly the whole way. Until we...stopped.

Cara stretches and sits up to peek at Margo's phone. "Nice. Over a million followers overnight. I'm sure it has nothing to do with being tagged in your famous best friend's wedding pictures."

Wedding pictures.

What. The. Fudge?

I jolt upright and pry Margo's phone from her hand.

No. No. No. No. No. No.

Right there on the screen in all our bright and technicolor Christmas glory is Jaden and I sealing our vows with a kiss in front of an Elvis-impersonating officiant in red and green crushed velvet. *Crushed velvet!*

My mind scrambles, and the first thing I think about is how the scandal will affect my chances for the tour.

I swallow, frantically zooming in for some hint the photo's been doctored or photoshopped. Nothing. Just the five of us tagged along with the Gold Band Chapel in Las Vegas, Nevada. *Why would Margo tag me?*

And then there's the caption.

Married and Bright.

#Loveatfirstsilentnight #homeforchristmas #rideointothedistance #bliss&makeupco #crimsonqueen #specialeditionblissweddingplanner #caraabouthair#loveisintheair #tistheseason #BiancaandJaden #winterwonderland #irishguysarehot #blameitonthehotchocolateshots #goldbandchapel

I lower my chin and stare at the thin gold ring on my left hand.

Fuck. Fuckety. Fuck. Fuck.

I can't. I will not look at my phone right now.

We had such an amazing time last night, and now everyone will pick it apart. Just thinking about how many messages I probably have sends my mind into overdrive. *Mom.* Another part of my life she's been left out of. Damien's probably shitting a brick and going into full damage control mode with Museik. *Ugh.*

I don't even want to think about social media…

The tabloids are probably having a field day with this one.

My hands itch to tap on my profile on Margo's phone. If I could just see how bad it is, maybe…

I take a deep breath, counting to ten in my head. *Don't do it, Bianca.* I have to get some perspective. *Three, four, five…* Figure out how to explain this away.

Why did they tag me? I should have insisted on no pictures. *Six, seven…*

It feels like minutes go by before I lift my eyes to my friends'.

Breathe. Eight, nine…

"How did this happen?" I try to keep my voice even, but it comes out shaky, streaked with a mix of panic and misplaced anger. "My manager's trying to get me on tour…"

Cara, Margo, and Denise turn to face me. Their eyes are wide and unblinking, their shoulders tense as they survey me.

"Breathe," Cara says softly, gently taking the phone from my hand. "It's not the best, but it's publicity. I'm sure it's going to be fine. Just stay away from social for a little while. It'll blow over. For now, whatever you want to do, we'll help with the damage control."

Margo softly touches my arm, letting her hand rest on my pulsing skin. She opens her mouth to speak but immediately closes it again. Then her eyes dart behind me.

I don't have to turn to know Jaden is awake. I feel the slight shift in the mattress as he sits up, and I can't turn to face him.

"Don't worry. We wouldn't want you attached to a nobody like me." His tone is a hard shell over hurt, and I feel a pang of guilt tighten my chest. "We'll get a quickie annulment and you can get back to living your life in the spotlight."

I scrub a hand over my face, letting my head rest in my palm.

How is this my life?

THE GOOD NEWS IS DENISE LIVES IN A DOWNTOWN LUXURY apartment with a terrace and private parking. With an aerial view of their stakeouts, we're prepared for the paparazzi when we drive away. The bad news? With all the busy one-way streets, we don't get very far.

They're camped out on every street, and after a few phone calls to Bianca's mom and my older brother Eric, we've got no escape plan.

"Hold your jackets up to the windows," I say, carefully changing lanes, but not before the sea of cameras lurch toward the car.

I swerve in a near-miss with one of the photographers. Adrenaline surges through my veins and my heartbeat pounds in my ears.

"You're going to need black-out windows," Cara says, clutching the "oh-shit bar" as the car jerks with the speed.

For almost three minutes, we're sitting ducks forced to shield ourselves with our jackets until the light changes. I floor it to the freeway entrance, letting my breathing even out with the straightaway. Once we're safely out of reach, we all breathe a sigh of relief.

"Look, the two of us don't mind the heat. It's actually great for our businesses," Margo reasons, happy to share the spotlight with Cara, whose hair salon, Cara About Hair is now booked six months out.

"First, drop us off at my car." She instructs. "We'll do something outrageous to take some of the attention off of you…long enough for you to call Damien," she says to Bianca, who nods obediently. "Have him find a low-key place for you two to hole up for a few days."

You two.

Days.

I flit a quick glance over to Bianca, whose curved shoulders and lowered chin let on she's just as put out by Margo's impromptu plan to save her music career as she is about our marriage.

Last night, I was all for the plan. This was supposed to be fun. We'd both let loose and enjoyed ourselves. We're supposed to get the marriage annulled today. But I didn't expect to feel…anything.

For once, I'd let loose with a beautiful woman. I acted, *almost* without overanalyzing the risk factors and what it all added up to. It wasn't the one-night stand, it was *better*. Like a magnet, I was drawn to the lightness of Bianca's laugh and the warmth of her smile. I wanted more than just sex.

Stupidly, I let myself believe this was more than her having fun while she's in town for two weeks. *She's leaving, asshole. Don't read anymore into it.*

"Look, don't take this the wrong way. Last night was fun. We all had a great time, but I'm sure Bianca has more important things to do," I say. I flip on my blinker and move into the far-right lane. "I can push my schedule today, but this is the end of the fiscal year. It's not as exciting as having a song at the top of the charts, but I do have tax clients who need me.

"Yeah," Bianca quickly agrees, pulling out her phone.

Even though it was my idea not to prolong this any further, a small protest on her part would have lessened the blow to my ego.

"You're probably right," she says, unlocking the phone screen. She taps a few keys before pressing it to her ear.

Cara leans between the front seats to rub Bianca's arm as she pastes on a smile to talk. "Dame, it's me…"

Fifteen minutes later, true to their words, Margo and Cara make an outrageous scene as we drop them off. Wearing, sky-high heels and the now-famous Crimson Queen lipstick, they strut the street like it's their personal catwalk, twirling, dancing, posing for the paps.

As we drive off in the opposite direction with a wave, Bianca clears her throat and turns to face me. Like she did last night, and I'm pulled back into the same familiar, easiness I'd felt talking to her.

"I'm sorry," she says sheepishly, and I'm surprised because I'm not sure what she's apologizing for. "I swear I wasn't trying to be rude to you back there at Denise's. You've been nothing but kind to me and my friends, and we had an amazing time."

"No, it's okay. We just had a wild night." I flash her a smile before returning my eyes back to the road.

"I just want you to know, I don't regret any of it. I just… I'm pretty private about my personal life. Having everyone comment on us, editorializing our perfect night... It's kind of overwhelming for me."

I'm trying to keep an even mind about all of this, but I can't discount how hearing her describe last night as perfect buoys my spirits.

I feel the tension in my shoulders drain slightly.

With a quick glance over at her, I note there's nothing but remorse and empathy in her expression.

"Definitely. I get that. It's probably hard having everything you do end up in a tabloid or on a trending list."

I make a left turn, driving aimlessly because I'm not sure where we're going. "Look, I'm sorry about last night. I shouldn't have been so flippant about getting married given your career." I slouch into the seat, adjusting my hands down on the steering wheel. "People don't just meet, get married, and stay married just because they had a perfect night, right?"

I toss her a small smile.

Her eyes are alight with an arresting calm.

As the walls we erected since last begin to crack, I get a glimpse of the same heat that pooled in her gaze at O'Sullivan's.

I avert my gaze anyway.

It was one night together. It doesn't mean anything.

Her phone pings, and she checks the message. "Damien sent the address. He got us a private villa at The Mansion."

My eyes snap to hers. "Us?"

I hate the way my heart slows to a languid thud against my chest.

"He's sending a runner to Mom's for me. If you want, he'll have someone pick up whatever you need, too."

"Won't it just make things worse for you if we're tucked

away together?" I'm still trying to get a handle on where her head is. "The paparazzi will eat this up."

She lifts her hand and glides it over the back of my neck, blazing a strangely familiar trail over my skin. Her warm fingers weave into my hair. It takes everything in me not to lean into her touch.

"Neither of us signed up for this media storm, Jaden. I was thinking, maybe we could weather it together..." she says, sinking her teeth into her lower lip. "What kind of wife leaves her husband out in the rain?"

"A smart one?" I chuckle, keeping my eyes on the road.

But Bianca doesn't laugh. She removes my right hand from the steering wheel, taking it in hers.

When she lifts her head, I want to tell her how she unnerves me and makes my heart stutter, and that even though I'm scared as hell, and everything about our lives feels like a mismatch, I went into this marriage sober because I wanted this adventure with her. *Even if it comes with an expiration date.*

Instead, I return my eyes to the road, lace our fingers, and give her hand a reassuring squeeze.

THE GRAPEVINE

The Rideo driver who nabbed the holiday songstress

WHO IS JADEN BROOKS?

Inside the chart-topping pop star's wild Vegas night that ended at a downtown chapel. Where are the newlyweds now?

BIANCA MARRIED!

O'SULLIVAN'S

SINCE 1983

MEET ST. PADDY CLAUS

FUN GREEN WIGS

ENJOY A **DRINK** ON US

HOT CHOCOLATE SHOTS * LAGER

#1 single

Mistletoe Memories

Bianca

Damien's runners meet us in a grocery store parking lot off The Strip. From there, we're chauffeured through a private drive directly to our honeymoon villa, where a tall, beefy guy in a black suit named Omar now stands guard at our door.

"Is this always how it is for you?" Jaden asks, scrubbing a nervous hand over his face. "VIP all the way?"

I shrug. "When I'm not the main headline, I can usually get away with a black cap pulled low over my eyes and a fake name." I wink at him as I walk around checking out the rest of the space.

Our villa is Tuscan-themed with lots of stately wooden furniture and lush beige and gold fabrics. Every room has a chandelier. There's a beautiful crystal drop-tiered one above the bed in the huge master.

Perfect for couples who want…light.

As Jaden enters the room, I turn to absently rifle through the brochures and magazines on the nightstand, and my mind wanders to fun things Jaden and I could do with that chandelier.

The squeak of the mattress coils snags my attention and I toss a look over my shoulder.

Jaden's hand is pressed into the layers of down comforter and crisp sheets like he's testing for firmness. He stops when he catches me sizing him up.

Actually, I'm gawking.

Gah, act like you've been in a bedroom with a man this decade. Even if it that's how long it's been since sex has been any good.

"Why are hotel beds always so much better?" He muses as he studies me. His eyes flicker with heat, but the corner of his mouth hitches up.

Please let him be as good as he looks.

I edge past him and work my way around to the terrace. It opens with direct access to a stunning Italian garden. It's private and gorgeous—the only way to do it if you have to go into hiding.

"Everything's better when you're in a gorgeous hotel." I agree.

For a moment, I soak up the sun and the sweet floral perfume. It feels like the hidden paradise I've been dreaming about—a getaway from all the hustle and bustle of life. It's an escape—beautiful sites, comfort—with someone who's made my heart beat again.

It's all here.

I've wanted and dreamed about it. I just never thought I'd get it.

Locking the French doors, I move on to the huge bathroom. "Hello!" I call out in complete appreciation and awe of the formidable jet stream tub at the center of the room.

"Hello, indeed," Jaden says as he walks up from behind me, surprising me as his arms encircle my waist.

My breath hitches, and my pulse speeds up.

It's so unexpected in the best way. I haven't been touched, kissed, or desired by a man who turns me on with his mere proximity in…ever. The funny thing is, there are always men around—attractive or not—but, I don't know who to trust, so I trust no one. I want to be free with Jaden.

I want to see what that glint in his eyes means.

"Oh, and there're bath bombs!" I all but break out into happy tears.

He rests his chin on the crown of my head. "Sounds relaxing."

For a split second, as we stare at the massive jacuzzi tub, and Jaden's arms are around me, I don't feel like I'm being hunted by paparazzi and forced to cut myself off from the world. I'm not hanging on to the chance to go on tour. *Everything* is *better in this hotel.* Standing here with the sweetest, sexiest man makes me wish this was all real—that we planned this marriage, and our honeymoon is more than just an accident.

I want it to be more than "one night in Vegas."

It's actually two weeks. *Would it be so bad if we played along for a little while?*

Clearly, I had a few drinks last night, but what if my subconscious knows something I don't? Other than alcohol and the fact he magically looks hotter by the second, there has to be a reason I said yes. We didn't have sex or share a bunch of drunken "I love yous." I don't think it's infatuation. So, what if it's rare for a CPA Rideo driver and a singer to find a happily ever after a quickie Vegas wedding? It could work…

If it doesn't, it's not like annulments are only good within the first twenty-four hours…

Are they?

I'm holding my breath, and my heart is in my throat. Gathering my nerves, I twist around to face Jaden.

The corners of his big brown eyes crinkle and his mouth quirks up. "What's going on in that head of yours?"

Take a deep breath.

I swallow "I know how this is *supposed* to end, but—"

A knock at the door echoes off the walls and I lose my train of thought. Worse, it feels like a sign stopping me from doing something incredibly stupid. Of course, he wouldn't want to stay married. I blame the holidays. That dang Winter Wonderland! I'm caught up in the fairytale.

It was probably just a crazy thing we did while we were drunk and living in a Hallmark Christmas movie for a night.

His face contorts in question.

Not to worry…just a bunch of hormones and emotions mixing over here. None of this is real. Like you said, people don't meet, get married, and stay married just because of a perfect night.

No matter what the season.

"I should probably get that," I say, swallowing my words as I edge past Jaden.

When I reach the door, I breathe out a relieved sigh. *That was a close one.*

Bianca stands on her toes to look through the peephole then pulls the door open. On the other side is Omar. All my focus centers on the box in his hands. It's huge and gold with an even bigger red ribbon.

"From Damien Eisner," he says simply.

She shoots him a questioning look, but as a man of few words, that's all she gets out of him. With a quick thank you, Bianca hefts the box inside, shaking it curiously as she walks over to set it on the living room table.

When she doesn't pick up our conversation where we left off, I'm a bit disappointed, but I take my cue from her.

"What'd you get?" I jerk my chin toward the box. "Early Christmas present?"

Omar said it was from her manager, but she still checks the tag.

"Actually…it's for us. A wedding gift from Damien." Bianca flips the tag to me. In bold red calligraphic script, it reads, "To Mr. and Mrs. Brooks."

I flick my gaze upward playfully.

"Want to help me open it, Mr. Brooks?" She winks.

I scratch my scalp and dip my chin to my chest, stifling a laugh. The fact that I like the idea of Bianca being addressed as Mrs. Brooks surprises me. For so long, getting serious with a woman felt pointless. Why even try when I need to put all my focus and energy into my family who *needs* me? Until I don't have to, my wants will come second.

It had always seemed unfair that a woman would only have access to half of me.

With Bianca, though, I want to know what it would be like to give more…feel more.

I join her at the table and unravel the ribbon. She slips off the lid.

There's a single gold envelope atop the layers of red tissue paper. For a moment, we both just stare at it. It's so fancy and sleek. Everything about it looks expensive, and I have no idea what to expect. To be honest, it feels wrong to open it when this marriage has an expiration date.

Bianca plucks the envelope out. "Always read the card

first," she says, tucking a wavy dark strand behind her ear. She tosses me a shaky smile.

I step to her side to read along and glide my hand to the small of her back as we scan the card.

Congratulations Mr. and Mrs. Brooks on your nuptials.

You did it! And now you want to undo it...

In order to maintain what little confidentiality we have left during this festive occasion, I'm using a private company to facilitate your annulment. As such, it will take some time, but I'll have it ready for you to sign when we meet in person at the Snowball Jam on Christmas Day.

Until then, enjoy your private villa. I've loaded you up with an array of items to accommodate your boredom. Maybe this time, you'll stay under the radar as previously advised. As I'm sure you'd be disappointed not to be with your families during the holidays, I've also provided an unlisted phone and a driver to arrange pickups and drop-offs. You know how to reach me in the event of emergencies. Best wishes on your not-at-all-low-key marriage.

Yours truly,

Damien Eisner

Bianca sets the card on the table. Her smile is soft and tentative. "You want to do the honors?"

Even though I couldn't care less what's in this box, and I'm dying for her to finish the thought she left hanging in the air, I remove the tissue paper quickly and in bunches.

"See? This is why he's not just my manager." Bianca

laughs and starts digging through a hodgepodge of Christmas—and marriage—themed items. "He's like a quirky friend and the weird older brother I never knew I wanted."

There's a gingerbread house kit, a Bliss & Makeup Co. special edition wedding planner, a dozen Christmas movies, and sweets. Bianca must have a sweet tooth. There's candy, double chocolate fudge, and sugar cookies. He also included classic board games, a card making set, and an old Polaroid camera…to mark the occasion, I'm guessing.

"He's thorough. I'll give him that," I say, but she's still digging through items on the bottom of the box, and her eyes sparkle with excitement.

This attraction I have for her is so natural and easy. How am I this comfortable with a person I've known less than twenty-four hours? What is it about her that something as simple as her opening a present turns me on?

I decide to leave Bianca to it and go plop down on the bed, crossing my ankles and clasping my hands behind my head. I study her, eager to understand the magnetism between us when I've spent so long pushing women away.

I'm lost in her silhouette. The shadows and contours of her sweeping curves and easy posture…the soft roundness of her breasts and the sway of her hips… her curls cascading over her shoulders…the sweet pout of her lips…

When Bianca finally lifts her head, she's beaming. She jerks her hand up, and she's holding a green piece of paper. She spots me looking at her and turns restless. Her free hand tightens into a fist before she loosens it again, flexing her fingers.

"You tired?" she asks.

"Nope."

Nipping the tip of her finger, she tries again. "Bored?"

"Definitely not."

I get a deep satisfaction to see her nervous under the weight of my stare.

She lifts her hair off her neck letting is spill down her back again. "Then what are you doing?" she asks sheepishly, taking measured steps toward me on the bed.

I let my gaze drift over her as she moves to the left side. "Enjoying watching my beautiful wife."

A blush grows on her cheeks.

I don't want to make her uncomfortable, so I shift my attention to the paper in her hands. "What's that you've got there?" I unclasp my hands and open my left arm, indicating for her lie beside me.

Bianca crawls into the crook of my arm and rests her head on my shoulder. "I thought this might be fun. 'Questions to Know if Your Marriage Will Last.'"

I tilt my head to look at her with a smile tugging at the corners of my mouth. "Are we already in trouble? Should we get therapy?" I chuckle.

She erupts with laughter.

"You think it's funny, but that's literally one of the questions." I hear the smile in her voice as she returns her focus to the paper. "Guess that takes care of this one. 'Willing to go to couples' therapy if needed.' Check. What about children?"

"What about them? They're small and smell funny, but they're all right, I guess."

Bianca tickles my side, and I twist away from her.

"I'm kidding, yes. If you're taking orders, let's go with two, well-adjusted ones to start. A boy and girl. We'll add more as desired."

"You're a bag of jokes today without your rescue mobile, aren't you?" She kicks off her shoes then crawls to the foot of the bed.

She starts to take mine off too, and the gesture steals my breath. It's both unanticipated and thoughtful...personal. She doesn't seem to notice how affectionate and caring it is. All the humor drains away.

I'm flooded with warmth filling a void I didn't know was there.

Her eyebrows furrow as she looks at me over her shoulder while still on her hands and knees. "What?"

My eyes dart from her, back to the paper. My pulse is racing. "Bianca, what were you going to say? Earlier, when we were in the bathroom, you said you know how this is supposed to end. But what were you going to say next?"

She stills, and her shoulders stiffen. When I don't let her off the hook, she hedges.

"Nothing." She waves it off, but there's no conviction in her tone.

I study her for a few seconds. "Please. I really want to know."

Sitting back on her knees, Bianca drops her chin to her chest. "You'll think it's crazy."

"I promise, I won't."

She's quiet for a short while, and I don't press her. Then, she gives me a sidelong glance. "I just...when you mentioned the quickie annulment in the car, I went along with it because I figured that's what you wanted. Damien assumed, too, so he got right to work to undo everything."

I nod.

"It's like everyone has an idea how this should end."

"But?" I probe, sitting up. I chuck up her chin so I can see her warm brown eyes and read the truth in them.

"What if we didn't get an annulment?"

She's searching my face, waiting for the other shoe to drop. When it doesn't, she continues.

"At least not in the next two weeks just because that's what we're *supposed* to do, or because that's when I'm scheduled to leave. What if we got to know each other and tried this out?" The hope lifting her shoulders buoys my spirits. "That's what dating is, anyway…trying each other on for size and seeing if we fit." She laughs.

I lay a gentle hand to her arm, swiping the pad of my thumb over her smooth skin as she shakes her head at herself.

"I'm pretty sure I just paraphrased Tom Hanks in *Sleepless in Seattle*, but it's true."

My heartbeat speeds up, and my throat tightens. I don't know what to say. I mean, I know how I feel, but is it enough? Is any of this real, or are we just caught up in a wonderful moment? *Could we do this?*

"But you *are* leaving, Bianca. Doesn't it seem pointless to start something we may not be able to finish?"

She nods. "I know, but I don't even have a contract for the tour yet. What if I don't get it? That's gambling on an unknown, too."

I chew on the inside of my cheek, weighing her words. "So, what are you saying?" I ask, needing to hear her lay it out for me and grateful she's not stuck on "the end," either.

"I'm saying we obviously have crazy chemistry. We both eventually want kids." This time the laugh that erupts from her is a soft melody, lulling me into this crazy whirlwind that's swept us away. "You've already checked 'couples' therapy as needed' off the list."

She's still ticking items off on her fingers, proving a case. I've already come to an incredible verdict. It makes no sense, but nothing about what we're feeling is based in logic…

"What if we didn't end this just because we did things backward?"

"Backward?" I chuckle. "My older brother, Eric, he always says nothing is worth trying unless you've tried it backward first."

She scrunches her face. "He sounds like a lot of fun."

"He is," I say, thinking about Eric and his silver linings outlook on life. "You'll have to be on your A-game when you meet him." *When?*

As soon as the words are out of my mouth, I stiffen. My pulse quickens, and my muscles tense. I feel myself sinking deeper into this quicksand. Meeting family, making plans, it implies so much more. It's presumptuous, foolish.

"I'm looking forward to it." A ghost of a smile crosses her face.

The tension drains from my body.

"Anyway, not all the way backward, we didn't start with the baby in the baby carriage." She giggles.

I cup her face in my hands. "Let me get this straight. Are you telling me you want to marry me, Mrs. Brooks?" I ask, pulling my lower lip between my teeth.

"Technically, we're already married, but yes. It'll be like one of those instant marriage reality shows where they get to know each other after they've said, 'I do,'" Bianca reasons. "I want to be your wife. I want you to be my husband, so I can call you something syrupy sweet like Boo Boo Bear."

I release a short bark of laughter. I feel weightless.

"If you don't freak out on me, I want to take off your shoes for you like my mom did for my dad. She didn't do it because she had to but because she wanted to show him how she felt with her actions."

"I'd like that."

Bianca squeezes her eyes shut. "Hopefully, at some point we can take a shower before another forty-eight hours passes."

I swallow at all the enticing images that come with the word "we."

Gently, I lean in to cover her full pillowy lips with mine. The kiss is unhurried and all-consuming. I dip my tongue into her mouth, teasing her tongue, tasting this sweet woman who is happy to be mine.

"What's your middle name?" I ask.

"Reina."

"Queen?" I ask between kisses. She nods and looks at me inquisitively, like she's shocked I know Spanish. "My queen."

Bianca glides her hands over my chest, pulling me closer. "Is that a yes, Mr. Brooks?"

"Yes. I agree to date my wife." I pull back to look at her. "You go enjoy the jacuzzi tub. I'll order room service." *And rub one out really quick.* "Then, if you're game, I say we go full force on that gingerbread house."

Bouncing off the bed, she backs into the bathroom. "You, Mr. Brooks, have yourself a deal."

THE GRAPEVINE

The bestselling lipstick you never knew you needed

CRIMSON QUEEN

Bliss & Makeup Co.
Margo Lavine, CEO

YOU CAN HIDE BUT YOU CAN'T RUN

Last seen with her new husband, Rideo driver, Jaden Brooks, pop star Bianca dodges photographers. Get all the details about the bars they were seen leaving, what they drank, and where you can get a fun green wig, too.

SNOWBALL JAM

LOVESTRUCK
DETAILS FROM THE HOLIDAY MIX ' N 'MINGLE
BROUGHT TO YOU BY THE WORLD'S MOST POPULAR SOCIAL DATING APP

WIN A BLISS & MAKEUP CO. SPECIAL EDITION WEDDING PLANNER!
*Details inside.

CHAPTER SIX

Something magical happens when you add fun and games into a relationship. I'm not just talking sex, either. Although, my nerves tingle every time I think about when Jaden and I will finally getting to the "good part." I'm literally referring to the games we've played from Damien's box of goodies and how they've made this marriage more real than I could've imagined three days ago.

It's Sunday. We spent the morning sledding at Mt. Charleston. We played in the snow, for the second time this week, like kids. I haven't laughed or played this much... ever. Because we're really digging our heels into this play-and-talk-until-we-know-each-other process, we've just finishing up another sheet of Yahtzee—in bed with hot chocolate. *Real hot chocolate!*

How can life get better than this?

"Roll, Snow Queen," Jaden says using one of his many terms of endearment he's come up with for me these past few days.

I've also been Queen, Reina, Mrs. Paddy Claus, and Sugar Bear. My favorite, though, is "Mrs. Bone Collector."

Naturally, I'm lying on my side with my head propped on my elbow, staring at him like a ninny again because he's so dang adorable.

Jaden leans forward to muss my hair and quickly brush his lips over mine. As familiar as his kiss has become, I'm still overwhelmed electrified by the feel of him and my feelings for him.

It's surreal to be someone's wife.

I sigh just taking in all this goodness.

Reluctantly, I shake the cup and let my dice spill out onto the Monopoly game board we're using for a hard surface.

Four fives and a six.

I should be checking my score sheet, deciding whether to go for the Yahtzee, four-of-a-kind, or extra points at my top, but I'm so lost in my husband—his company, his honey brown eyes and his easy posture. He's let me set the pace physically, but every second I'm near him, I feel my willpower waning.

Lying in bed with him and kissing him night after night makes me want more.

"Bianca," he says, lowering his chin to look at me from beneath his eyebrows. "Do I want to know what you're thinking?" A lopsided grin tugs at the corner of his mouth.

Heat gathers low and tight in my belly. Because even the slight gruff to his voice sets my skin on fire, I don't say a word to interrupt.

I nod.

Methodically, I slide the game board to the nightstand and remove his scorecard and pencil from his hand.

"Don't be a sour loser," he says jokingly.

I flash him a soft smile and bite my lower lip. "Mr.

Brooks," I say as I crawl in front of him, tugging the hem of his shirt up. "Yesterday, you met my mother and somehow charmed her into making the Christmas fudge bars she hasn't made since my dad died. We've slept beside each other every night since we met, and you haven't touched me…"

Jaden lifts his arms as I tug his shirt over his head. After I toss it off the side of the bed, he stares at me without blinking as he processes my actions.

"How long has your dad been gone?" he asks. His tone is filled with empathy, but he won't let me get away with brushing over the hard stuff.

I let my chin drop to my chest as the weight I've been carrying levels on my shoulders. He tips my chin up to look in my eyes.

"You don't have to tell me, B."

I shake my head because I want to tell Jaden. I want him to know everything about me the same way I want to know him, but it's hard letting people in.

"It's not that." I feel the familiar sting at the corners of my eyes. My heart wrenching. "I want to tell you, but…I haven't talked about him to anyone."

Jaden glides his hand over the curve of my cheek. "It's okay. Take your time."

And I do. I let the memories of Mom and me outside his hospital room course through my veins. The doctor's careful tone replays in my head. "The injuries sustained to his spinal cord in the accident were too great." *Losing him was too great.*

"We lost him five and a half years ago," I hear myself say, but it's almost like I'm someone else hearing it for the first time. Saying it aloud makes it real. I chew on my bottom lip. "After, I spent all my time in the studio. I couldn't bear to be home. I felt him in every inch of space, but *he* wasn't there."

Jaden pulls me against his warm, hard chest, and his hands comfort me.

Wrapped up in his clean, calming scent, I let the tears spill over.

With every word I tell him, I feel our threads crossing and weaving our bond tighter. Since Jaden came into my life, I've been reacting without taking action. But him listening and holding me while I tell him what plagues me most makes me feel like we really can do this together.

Bianca twines our fingers, anchoring us.

"A couple of months after he died, when I'd gotten my first contract, I just left. I didn't want to leave Mom or my friends, and I know it was selfish of me, but I needed to get away and not think about home anymore, if that makes sense."

I lift our hands to my lips and kiss the back of hers. "I get it. You were coping with an unimaginable loss."

My heartbeat stutters with each labored breath, and my chest tightens.

Bianca and I have been playing roles up until now… playing house. We've definitely enjoyed each other's company, but we've only just scratched the surface. Hearing her pour her heart out makes me want to go deeper, though. I don't mind being honest and vulnerable if it'll help us grow closer.

Massaging her back, I kiss the crown of her head.

"In an instant your whole life changes."

She must register the familiar weight of my voice. "Your dad, too?"

I shake my head. "My brother, Eric. He's still with us, but

he's not well."

Bianca snuggles into me.

"He's older than I am, but we're close. We'd talked about traveling together once I'd finished college, gotten a job, and been in the workforce a while. We were going to see the world…a brother's trip."

She tilts her head up, and her touch softens on my skin.

"That was a few years back. We'd planned a Mediterranean cruise—France, Spain and Greece. I'd saved up, mapped out all the landmarks, and even downloaded a language app." The laugh doesn't make it past my lips. "Then Eric got diagnosed with ALS."

Bianca kisses my chin and I lean into her warmth.

"We were still going to go, but my parents were too worried. Then all the medical bills started to pile up, and the whole family pulled together. On top of my day job, I drive for Rideo to make extra money to help."

I shrug though nothing about my brother's battle has ever felt light.

"I want to run away from it sometimes, but I stay. If Eric can keep fighting tooth and nail through this disease, the least I can do is be by his side." My jaw tightens as I bite back the emotion gripping my throat. "It makes me feel like such an asshole to dream and think about going off somewhere without him when he's fighting for his life."

I squeeze my eyes closed, lowering my head to pinch the bridge of my nose.

Bianca shifts in my arms, lifting her mouth to mine.

"It makes you human," she whispers between kisses. "It makes you a good brother and the kind of man who puts his family first. There's nothing wrong with that."

Gently, she cups my face with her delicate hands and presses her forehead to mine.

"It makes you the man I want to be married to."

I'm flooded with warmth, and my skin blazes beneath her touch. I need to be closer. Tugging at her, I kiss her hungrily.

The heat of my sadness flickers into desire. I glide my fingers into her hair, and my breath comes faster.

Then Bianca pulls away and vaults off the bed. She holds up her hands. "Hold that thought, babe."

"Okay," I say with an emotion-choked laugh.

I'm rock hard and sensitive, and she's...*what is she doing?*

From the other room, I hear her shuffling and tissue paper swishing.

Is she really digging in the Christmas box now?

Less than a minute later, Bianca comes running back to the bed with her hands hidden behind her back.

"If it's another board game, I'm really not in the mood." I say, scrubbing a hand over my face with an amused sigh. "There's nothing in that box I want right now."

Bianca cocks her head, and a smirk curls her upper lip.

"Are you sure about that?" With a little shimmy dance that makes me laugh, she swings her hands around.

I immediately start laughing because nothing could have prepared me for the festive box of condoms in both red *and* green colors—jolly peppermint flavor or cheerful chocolate "to add holiday spirit while amplifying the lovemaking experience."

You can't make this stuff up.

"That Damien..." I shake my head and laugh. "I have to hand it to him. He really did think of everything."

I look up at my sexy wife. Lust glitters in her eyes, draining all the humor from the moment. She stares at me as she tears the condom box open with her teeth.

Fuck.

"You're sure you want to do this?" *With me?*

Pinching a jolly peppermint red condom between her fingers, she licks her lips. "I'm one hundred percent sure I want to use every last one of these with my *ridiculously sweet, decent, devastatingly hot* husband," she says, emphasizing each word.

She sets the condom down on the bed, and we tug at each other's clothes until almost every stitch of fabric between us is gone.

I let my gaze move along her soft curves.

"*Fuck.*" I breathe the word because I'm trying to tamp down my arousal. I can't see how I'll be able to when all I want to do is bury myself into her. I want to feel her writhing beneath me and moaning her satisfaction.

"Don't move," Bianca instructs, climbing onto the mattress.

She grabs the condom and crawls toward me until we're both on our knees, facing each other. With her tongue, she blazes a trail a heat over my chest with peppering kisses and licks, coaxing a hungry growl from me.

Every nerve ending in my body tingles and stirs. My dick throbs in anticipation as she hooks her thumbs over the waistband of my boxer briefs, tugging them down around my knees.

I scrape my fingers over my scalp, clasping my hands behind my head. "I need to touch you, Bianca."

"Not yet. Just close your eyes."

With a frustrated sigh, I shut them. Now I experience her with all my other senses. I hear the crinkling as she rips the wrapper off the condom. I feel her warm hands on my shaft as she glides the condom over the length of my erection. The minty smell heightens my anticipation.

"I want to show you how sure I am," she whispers.

Then I feel searing, wet heat as her lips cover my dick in a long, aching stroke. Her teeth lightly graze my sensitive skin. Then her hands and mouth alternate pumping and sucking. Her actions are fast and hard as she moves her lips to the tip before taking me whole in her mouth again.

A jolt of electricity ripples through me, and I'm blindsided with lust. Every inch of my flesh tingles as desire flickers to life inside me.

"Oh my…fuck."

When she brings her hands around me and grips my ass to take me deeper, every muscle in my body constricts.

She moans, and it almost sends me over the edge. A tattered growl escapes my lips. All the sexual tension that's been building between us the past three days releases all at once.

"I want you come with me, baby," I say through shallow breaths, opening my eyes and pulling her up by her shoulders. I need to feel her breasts and her heartbeat flush against me as I move inside her tight pussy.

She lies on her back, letting her knees hang open, I battle the dueling distractions of her pliant body and the slightly more daunting feat of trying not to come. She's so beautiful and feminine, it's overwhelming.

I place the blunt head of my length between her thighs and thrust my hips until a gasp pushes past her lips.

She arches her head back, baring the delicate curve of her neck to me.

"Fuck," I groan, but I can't move.

It's too good. That's my first thought. I don't want to move an inch. I'm breathless. Speechless. All coherent communication is lost in the feel of her wet sex tight around me.

"What's wrong?" Bianca asks, with concern on her face.

Oh, you have it so wrong. Nothing could be more right.

For me, sex is usually a race of strokes and thrusts to bring about climax. With Bianca, I want to last. I don't ever want it to be over with. I just want to stay like this. My mind and body are wholly consumed by the feel and the teasing essence of my wife.

"Let's just stay like this. I could prop pillows under us…"

Her eyes flutter open and she giggles.

"I'm serious. I've saved up a lot of money. We can live in this villa forever and never leave."

Bianca weaves her fingers into my hair and raises up to kiss me.

I slide my hand up the smooth skin of her inner thigh to twist her sensitive bud. Her lips part and her answering moan sends heat swarming over my body. My heart rate revs up, and I release a low growl.

"I don't know how I got on the 'nice' list but I'm a new fan of flavored condoms," I say, nuzzling her neck and nipping behind her ear.

This time, she erupts into a fit of laughter, and the sound is so warm and musical, my cock jolts. She lifts her hips, writhing beneath me as I slowly find my rhythm. Holding my weight over Bianca, I alternate between slow and steady strokes and hard and fast thrusts, gliding out to the tip each time. We shudder, molding our bodies to one another.

She clings to my arms, and her orgasm ripples through her. I let go.

I'm lost in the scent of her shampoo and the mint on her tongue. No matter what happens when these two weeks are over, I know she'll be imprinted in my memory just like this with her face twisted in ecstasy. My desire deepens for my wife as we hold each other. We're just two open hearts with no barriers or ticking clocks. Tasting her and teasing her tongue with mine, I know this is a Christmas miracle.

CHAPTER SEVEN

"What do you want to do today?" I ask, gathering handfuls of bubbles to cover myself as I slouch below the waterline to let the jets do their work.

Jaden leans into the tub basin and lifts my foot out of the water, tickling me. He nips at my toes.

"Behave." I widen my eyes at him, but I can't bite back the grin tugging at the corner of my mouth. "I could just add more hot water and stay in this jacuzzi tub…"

"You would like that," he says in mock exasperation.

A week ago, our first time together was a magical fantasy of peppermint-flavored condoms and back-to-back orgasms. I'd been wild and insatiable for Jaden. Today, I'm still ravenous for him, but we're growing into an easy comfort around each other. Our constant touches transmit whispers of longing, and I'm falling.

I'm so deep in this. It scares me because we're still in this villa—a safe bubble hidden from the real world. Other than phone calls from my girls, Mom, and Jaden's entire family, it's just the two of us.

I sink down into the now lukewarm water, letting it flood around my face. Gently, he glides his hands in wide strokes up and down my thigh.

Opening for him, I close my eyes. "Why? Did you have something in mind for today?"

He glides his hand between my thighs, swirling his fingers in a mind-numbing circle.

I rotate my hips, craving and needing him inside me.

"It can wait," he says, his voice gruff as he grips my hips, pulling me closer.

As much as I want love sex with Jaden, not knowing what he was going to say plays on my insecurity. Is he tired of the bubble?

"Babe?"

"Well, Eric..." He trails off, but now I'm even more worried. Especially when he mentions his brother.

I jolt upright, my breaths labored as I read the warring emotions in his expression.

"What it is? Is Eric okay?" The words rush out panicked, and my mind spirals. If he wasn't there for his family or his brother because of me... "Babe tell me. You're scaring me."

"Don't worry. It's nothing urgent. Eric's fine."

My shoulders relax, but Jaden's not looking at me. His chin rests on his chest and he blows out a heavy sigh before meeting my gaze.

"It's okay. You can tell me anything." My heart slows to a heavy thud.

"Well, for my family everything is a big deal." He chuckles to himself, and I feel the lightness spreading between us. "I don't know if you remember me telling you about it at O'Sullivan's, but..." He runs his fingers through his hair, squeezing his eyes closed.

"Jaden..."

"Tonight's my family's annual ugly sweater party, and if I don't go, they will never *ever* let me hear the end of it."

I survey my totally decent, clean-cut, nerdy husband. His *Dexter* haircut is mussed in wet spikes. His big brown eyes are expectant and fixed on me. A flush grows on his cool skin from his neck to his cheeks. *How is he so adorably sweet?*

My lips twitch as I bite back the giggle threatening to spill out.

"Don't laugh." He warns me, but it's too late.

I'm already sliding back under the water. The bubbles tell on me.

"If you don't want to attend the best ugly sweater party in the greater Las Vegas area, fine. You don't know what you're missing out on, though," he says, pulling me to the surface. When I come up with my lips still quivering with laughter, he waits.

"Okay, I'm done."

An easy smile twists the strong lines of his face. "In all seriousness, though, I've never brought anyone home. They're going to read everything into you being there."

"And you're sure you want me to be the first?"

Jaden seeks and finds my mouth, kissing me senseless. "One hundred percent."

"Well, okay, then."

I flash him a closed-mouth smile because my heart is too full to speak. If going to hang out with his family for a few hours in hideous Christmas knitwear earns me that kind of knee-weakening kiss, well, then, a girl's got to do what a girl's got to do.

Twenty minutes after I badger Jaden with questions

about his family, what types of things they do at the party, and what they know about me, it's decided. We'll wear stylish holiday knitwear selections picked up by Omar from the local discount department store. At seven sharp we'll arrive at Mrs. Brooks' house where I'll meet the whole lineup: Mrs. Brooks, the Christmas-obsessed matriarch; Mr. Brooks, the movie buff; Eric, the sports fan; Denise, the crazy cousin; and Aunt Sarah, the root of the family grapevine.

There will be food and alcohol followed promptly by an intense, high-stakes game of Christmas movie trivia, which I'm eagerly looking forward to.

Jaden paces around our villa making phone calls to confirm with his family. He double-checks the pickup and drop-off times.

Seeing him anxious and excited to see his family gives me a twinge of guilt. I've hardly spent any time with Mom.

I'll try again tomorrow.

At least we're getting out of this villa, even if it is to see Jaden's folks who know nothing about me except my name, and the fact I've kept Jaden away from them for ten days during the holidays. *Awesome.*

A few hours later, we're wearing matching red and green snowflake sweaters and holding hands in the backseat of a SUV. Omar's riding shotgun beside the super-serious driver. All and all, the drive is quiet—nerve-rackingly so—which is why I jump when my phone pings.

I lift my free hand to glance at the screen.

"It's just Damien," I say, tossing Jaden a shaky smile, but then I actually read the message.

Damien Eisner 6:38pm
Are you sitting? Remember the gig I said would take your career to the next level? You know, I mentioned it all the way

back before I told you to lay low, then you got married, causing a media storm. Well, you got it.

My mind spirals. How do I tell him I'm rethinking my whole future? What I thought I wanted may not be enough anymore.

Bianca Esposito 6:39pm
Well don't leave me hanging…

Damien Eisner 6:38pm
Museik is in. World tour. 100 dates so far. 50 on the European leg alone. This is it, B! Everything you've been working toward. What do you think?

Jaden leans over my shoulder and I feel myself angling the phone away from him.

Ten days ago, a global tour felt like the end-all-be-all. It was my career marker to let me know I'd made it. What recording artist doesn't dream about the *world* discovering her music? I still remember the first concert I attended and how surreal it felt to be sharing the same space with my favorite singer. But 100 dates, travel time between cities, rest days… I could be gone over a year.

Another year away from Mom, my girls, *my husband…*

It was my idea to give this marriage, however fleeting it might be, a real chance to see where it could go. Now what? Tell Jaden I was just kidding? I wanted to see where his head was at, but anything beyond these two weeks is out of the question?

Don't think about it now. We'll figure something out.

I lock the phone and set it on the seat. My pulse races, and heat swarms over my skin.

"Everything okay?" Jaden asks.

Swallowing, I flash him a tight smile. "Yeah. Yeah."

He squeezes my hand and presses his lips to my temple, calming me. His warmth and comfort soothe me, and I'm reminded of another dream—one I pushed to the back burner because it felt so out of reach. *It was a horrible reminder of how easily a family could be torn apart.*

This glimpse of happiness, these days Jaden and I have spent together, I can't ignore my yearning for a deeper connection. A husband, a house, a family, babies…

But the timing couldn't be worse.

I don't want to have to choose between my career and a real chance of love. *Is this love? Am I only allowed one dream?*

The driver turns into a gated community, providing the uniformed man in the security booth with the Brooks' address and our names. After a few moments, he confirms we're guests of Jaden's family and opens the gate for us.

As we curve into the winding road, I feel my eyes widen at the older custom homes with sprawling driveways and swaying palm trees. "Oh my gosh. Jaden, they're breathtaking!"

I'm confused. The size of these houses. They've got to be expensive. I thought Jaden had two jobs to help his family out financially.

My gaze falls on a "For Sale" sign posted in front of a modern mansion with double garages and a circular driveway. I try to subdue thoughts of Jaden and me building a life.

"I love this community."

He gazes out the window, his eyes following absently. "It's tight-knit and friendly. Mostly everyone's been here since it was built a few decades back. I think it's why my parents have stayed. The economy's done a number on the property values, but they paid the house off a while ago, which helps as far as Eric's bills go. But, it's their dream house," he says as the SUV comes to a stop in front of a modest—compared to the other sprawling homes—single-story house with character and charm.

The adorable porch spans the width of the house. Bright red poinsettias line the walkway leading up to the steps, and sparkly lights make it feel like a vibrant star in an otherwise dim sky. But it's the picturesque bay window that makes my heart clench. The Christmas tree is full of lights, ornaments, and keepsakes.

Around it, Jaden's family is gathered, peeking out at us.

All. Of. Them.

My throat tightens and the corners of my eyes sting with emotion. I never had a huge family. It was always Dad, Mom, and me—three buttons on a cozy lapel.

Then Mom and me.

"Babe? What's going on?" Jaden turns and glides his thumb over my cheek. "It's going to be fine. They're going to love you."

I try not to think about Mom and Dad and how we used to stay in our pajamas all day Christmas, opening presents and playing games. As long as I had them, I was still me—free and whole.

After Dad died, I closed off my heart, but I didn't realize that by closing it, I was keeping any chance of new love out, too.

A pang wrenches my heart.

"Your family is so beautiful." I sniffle, swiping at my tears. "They're so happy to see you and to be a part of your life."

"They're excited to meet you, too. They know you're important to me."

"I guess…I just miss this—the part where you just get to relax and be yourself with the people who love you most," I say, swiping at a tear that's spilled over.

Jaden pulls me into his chest, banding his arms around me. "You have someone who loves—" He trails off. I can't see his face, but I feel the way his arms stiffen, how his breathing stutters.

I pull back just enough to search his brown eyes glittering in the darkness.

He swallows like he's bracing himself to say more.

"Bianca…" His eyes dart to the front seat at Omar and the driver before he pins me with his sharp stare. "I don't know how this happened, how I got so lucky, or how any of it would work, but I'm falling for you." He breaths a heavy sigh like saying the words is physically demanding.

It feels like a weight lifts off my chest and it's replaced by a new one.

How can I even think about traveling the world on tour with Museik when my heart will be here?

I close my eyes and nod. "Me, too." I give a shaky laugh. "I'm falling for you too, Jaden."

The words are barely out of my mouth before his lips crash down on mine. Jaden cups my face with his hands, and I slip my hands around his waist. The kiss is slow, gentle, and different from every other kiss we've shared. He coaxes a moan out of me as we sink into the hungry nips and licks. His tongue teasing mine. It's more than our lips; it's our hearts and our minds coming together.

A loud rap on the window snaps us apart.

"They're in there making out." Denise's muffled voice blares through the glass. "I told you. They can't keep their hands off each other long enough to get out of the damn car."

Jaden and I laugh because she's right. Now Jaden's entire family knows it, too. They're all standing at the door waiting for us to exit the car.

"Should we get out?" I cringe, both dreading this moment and excited to meet each one of them.

Mr. and Mrs. Brooks are the cutest little couple with slightly grayed dark hair and perky noses. I just want to give them Claus couple costumes to finish off the image. Aunt Sarah and Denise have their faces pressed to the glass, but they're both spritely, beautiful women with enough curves, red lipstick, and sass to spare.

The only person missing is the one I'm dying to meet, Jaden's older brother, Eric. From the stories Jaden tells, I know I'm going to love him.

When we do get out of the car, my heart smiles as Jaden is pulled into an assembly line of hugs. But when they're done with him, all the focus lands on me. I extend a shaky hand, uncertain of how to greet them for the first time, but they stare at my outstretched hand for less than a second before I'm treated to the same heartwarming hug line.

I've just met them, but I know without a doubt I'm falling for them, too.

We're not in the house five minutes, and I can't stop smiling. For one, Jaden's invited my mom, which is the sweetest, most thoughtful thing anyone has ever done for me.

Mom and I hold each other for a bit, observing Jaden's family, and I know she feels it, too. They're relationship is loud, quirky, and fun-loving. The way they so unabashedly share so much love fills our Dad-sized void.

Mrs. Brooks, sporting the ugliest drunken llama sweater, is nitpicking about her immaculate Christmas shrine of wreaths and garland, her cinnamon-scented candles are at the center of a feast of turkey and colorful side dishes. Mr.

Brooks is in a Christmas tree sweater with ornaments and fuzzy balls all over it is. He couldn't care less that the angel tree topper is about to fall off. He's comfy on the couch arguing which holiday movie is the best of all time. He declares *It's a Wonderful Life* is hands down number one. All the while, Denise and Aunt Sarah—whose matching red jingle bell sweaters aren't the least ugly—are video-chatting with someone about Jaden and I getting hot and heavy in the SUV.

Finally, I see Eric, and I'm immediately drawn to him.

He's got the same tussled dark hair, sunny glow, and warm brown eyes, but his smile is a bit more boyish despite the hard lines of his face. He seems less likely to get married on a bender than to indulge in pranks. His sweater should win the award for most inappropriate—it's a *Christmas Story* leg lamp with plenty of strategically placed tinsel hair at the apex of the leg.

"I'm convinced you've picked the wrong brother," he says, good-naturedly, flashing me a devastatingly sweet and crooked smile, but there's a hint of sadness underneath the surface. He gestures for me to move his wheelchair between the couch and chair before patting the seat beside him on the far end of the couch.

Before I leave Mom's side, I clear my throat. "Mrs. Brooks, Mom said she'd be happy to help out in the kitchen."

Happy to have help, Mrs. Brooks murmurs her approval. Mom stares daggers at me.

I laugh it off as I walk over to sit with Eric.

The corners of his eyes crinkle. "Aren't you a sly one?"

I wink at him. "You know, I think you might be right," I say, edging into his side as Jaden returns from the kitchen where he's been helping his mother. "I definitely got the short end of the stick as far as brothers go. I should've been clearer about the 'dashing' part."

We both laugh, scooting closer.

Jaden sits on the arm of the couch, tugging me to his side. "Hey. I resent that," he says with a chuckle before glaring at Eric playfully. Watching them together, there's nothing artificial about the way they love on each other. "Besides, you're too late, big brother. This one's already got my heart."

Warmth and happiness flood my insides. Even as he says the words, I know as much as we joke, he's got mine, too.

Later, we all split up in teams to battle over a *Jeopardy*-style game of holiday movie trivia. The categories include St. Kris Kringle Santa Nick, Reindeer Games, Holy Holidays, and Mingle All the Way.

As Jaden and I sweep the holiday romance category without blinking twice, I feel my resolve waning. I can no more change the way I feel about Jaden and his family than I can change the rhythm of my heartbeat. The weirdest part about it is, despite my maybe-this-times and inklings of doubt, I don't want to change the way I feel about him because I want Jaden.

CHAPTER EIGHT

Monday morning back at the villa, Bianca is still reeling from our holiday movie trivia win, not only against Team Moms and Brooks, but also Team Silver-ish Bells. Seeing her at home with my family and our families together makes me more certain than ever that I want to give us a real shot.

"Come on. 'A pop star sings?'" I thought your dad was going to kill Eric when he said that."

Bianca looks at my reflection in the mirror. Her eyes are bright with amusement as she applies light pink blush to her cheeks.

"He yelled at him like twenty times. 'Every time a bell rings, an angel gets his wings. *Wings*,'" she says in a deep baritone as she impersonates Dad. "I thought I was going to die laughing."

"Yeah. They're always at each other throats. I think Eric gets a kick out of winding him up."

She puckers and glides on red lipstick, stifling a laugh. "You think?"

A wave of warmth floods my system.

I lean casually into the doorway with my arms crossed over my chest, captivated by this moment. *I have a wife.* The realization is both surreal and humbling. That night in the chapel, I had no way of knowing how much I would feel for her only a week later. She's so much more than I ever dreamed.

Bianca Reina Esposito—unofficially, Bianca "my queen" Brooks, a minor detail I hope to rectify as soon as we get around to it—is a dream.

She's bent over the sink with her face inches from the mirror. Her long, dark curls spill over her back. The soft curves of her breasts and ass are arched alluringly. The delicate lines of her neck...

I'm starting to know them by heart.

Over my shoulder, I toss a whimsical glance to the unmade bed. Every second we spend together, I'm falling deeper, and sinking into us. I know it's all a dream, and soon I'll wake up.

"What's that look about?" Bianca asks, pulling my attention back to her.

When I return my gaze to her, she lifts an eyebrow at me in the mirror. Her eyes glow with affection, and hints of a smile dance on her red lips.

My heart nearly stops. Every inch of me aches for this woman.

"I..." I trail off, uncertain how to express myself.

The expression on my face must bleed with worry because Bianca turns around to face me with a concerned look. "Babe, what?" She erases the distance between us until we're inches apart.

Her eyes dart back and forth, searching my face.

I unfold my arms and fish my hand into my pocket.

Before I can pull it out, I search her eyes, praying I'm not wrong. "Do you still want to be my wife? I mean, do you still want to *really* give us a try?"

She presses her hands to my chest. "I want this. I want you…" Her words die off, a breath left in her chest.

All I can think about is what she's not saying.

The weight of the silence wedges between us, and I lower my head. "It's okay. I understand."

"No. I don't think you can," she says, tipping my chin up. "This, you and me, I've never been more certain about anything or anyone. But we're in this safe bubble away from the world. We haven't faced the internet trolls and the cameras."

"I know."

"Babe, they're ruthless and they won't stop at anything or anyone to get a photo or a soundbite. It's this weird, sadistic game of tug-of-war where they build you up to tear you down."

I nod, imagining how hard it must be for her to be blinded by the limelight. *How lonely.*

"Jaden, I'm just worried about what'll happen when we leave the villa. They don't have boundaries. They won't stop at our families or old friends, and we're not allowed to react. They'll spin it whichever way stirs up the most controversy."

When Bianca doesn't say anything more, about me or us, I can't deny how it raises my hopes. She didn't say she couldn't love me. She's not worried about our ability to last. It's all external factors burning at her. But if she can handle the spotlight, I'm willing to endure the heat with her.

Straightening, I pull my hand from my pocket with a deep a breath.

"We can't hide forever, but when we do go out, I hope

you'll wear this." I open my hand to reveal my grandmother's simple diamond on a white gold band. "Mom gave it to me Saturday night. She said to give it to you if I felt it in my heart."

Bianca's eyes well up with tears. Her lips part, and she presses a hand over her heart and breathes my name like she needs to hear it to know this is real.

"I'm in love with you, Bianca. I've never felt this way, and I want to make this official." I kneel, holding the ring out to her and say, "L.A. isn't that far. Or, maybe we can buy a house."

Bianca nods, staring down at the ring.

"We can make it work. Please marry me and make me the luckiest man on the planet, my Reina."

She nods, holding her left hand out for me. As I slide on the ring, she leans into me, crashing her lips down on mine.

"I love you, too."

Just the sound of those words coming from her mouth warms my chest. I'm overwhelmed with joy and happiness. Giddy hope courses through me as I deepen the kiss.

Her tongue teases mine as I tighten my hands on her waist. "Can we just stay like this forever?"

Bianca's stomach croaks, and we both erupt with laughter.

"I'm guessing I'd better feed you first before we get started on 'happily ever after.'"

She pulls back to look at me, using her thumb to wipe at what I'm pretty sure is all the red lipstick she's missing.

"How about we *not* eat in the hotel today? Let's go somewhere on The Strip." She waggles her brows. "If we're going to test the heat, there's no better time than now."

"If you're game, I am too."

An hour later, we're beneath the Eiffel Tower at the Paris Hotel.

We dine on the outdoor patio at Hexx, a curbside Strip restaurant with bright orange umbrellas and even brighter striped yellow and white awnings that practically scream for locals, tourists, and paparazzi to look at us.

And they do.

No less than five dozen cameras are aimed at us while we take small, photogenic bites of plate-perfect burgers. We're not in a private dining room or even tucked away in the corner of the restaurant. We just sit out in the waning daylight, begging to be seen.

Why didn't we stay at the villa?

"So, you're really sure about this?" I ask, angling away from the cameras.

Bianca smiles her magazine-cover-ready smile and sips her water with her left hand skyward like a pro.

"It's a little late for that now, don't you think?" As if taunting them, she dangles her ring finger, the diamond glinting strobe lights off the flashes.

"Bianca, over here!" A man with a huge camera and a fluffy red Santa hat calls out over the mob of people.

A few more yell questions about her holiday plans and the green wig from the night at O'Sullivan's, but they're mostly conversational and careful not to push the limits.

Then a shaggy-looking guy in cargo shorts and a faded black T-shirt with his cap flipped backward appears. Right off the bat, I can tell he's ruthless and hungry for the exclusive. He charges the gate, stepping up onto it so that he's within arm's reach of us. He angles his camera right at Bianca's face then pulls back to examine his screen.

Every muscle in my body tenses. My pulse slams in my neck.

"How does it feel to be married?" He asks, snapping photos. The sound of the shutter clicks nonstop.

Bianca tosses the guy a soft smile.

"Just ignore them," she says through closed teeth.

Then, he crosses the line. "Bianca, any big news we should expect in the next nine months?"

Anger sears through me, and my temples throb with rage at the implication that we're only married because she's knocked up.

Before I think better of it, I'm up off my seat in a blur of fury. I lunge for him just as he snaps photo after photo of what I'm sure the headlines will read as "Bianca's Unhinged Husband."

The chatter and gasps around us are drowned out by my heart jackhammering against my chest. Every horrible synonym runs through my mind as the guy smirks at me, still clicking away.

Deranged.

Disturbed.

Manic.

I'm shaking, my blood boiling. My hands flex, aching to… But I can't touch him. It's what he wants.

I won't be the protective, lovesick husband who wants nothing more than to make Bianca happy for the rest of my life. I'll be labeled volatile, hot-tempered, and short-fused. Then I'll be slapped with a lawsuit.

The photographer hops down off the gate with his mouth curved in a satisfied smirk.

I'm an idiot who just proved to Bianca I'm not strong enough to ignore their baited attempts for a reaction.

Fuck.

After I leave enough money for our bill and a sizable tip, Omar, who's been waiting near the entrance ushers us back inside where we wait for him to call the driver around. The whole ride home—back to our safe villa—I'm cursing myself for falling into the trap because Bianca hasn't said a word.

She warned me, but I'm fairly certain I didn't pass the limelight test.

THE GRAPEVINE

25 WARNING SIGNS
OF AN ABUSIVE RELATIONSHIP

SNOWBALL JAM
CHRISTMAS DAY
WITH BIANCA

Winter Wonderland

DOWNTOWN LAS VEGAS

GET OUT!

SPECIAL SAFETY ISSUE

Why the pop star needs to heed the warning signs
Bianca's unhinged husband. Get all the details about Jaden Brooks' explosive confrontation with photographers on The Strip. Hear why restaurant patrons feared for their lives and some say Bianca might be preggers!!!

CREEPY ENCOUNTERS WITH RIDEO DRIVERS
THE RIDESHARE SAFETY CONVERSATION YOU NEED TO HEAR

Jaden and I didn't have sex last night. After we got home from Hexx, we didn't talk, either. We undressed and slid beneath the covers and layers of tension. Both of us were waiting for the other to say something first or to have a solution to a problem neither of us understands.

Where do we go from here? How do we make this work when we're from two different worlds?

I wake before Jaden. At the faint chime of my phone ringing in my purse on the TV stand, I drag myself out of bed, groggy and numb from crying myself to sleep.

Seeing that it's Damien, I answer and tiptoe into the living room.

"Hey." I whisper, tossing a glance back at Jaden who's still curled in the blankets. "What's going on?"

"Let's see." Damien's tone is measured and tight, and I can tell he's pissed I've haven't gotten back to him about the tour. "It's Tuesday. I texted you with career-changing news on Saturday, and I've heard nothing back. On top of Museik,

I have another offer for a residency at a Strip hotel, but I haven't been able to tell you about it because you're making headlines again…"

He pauses for brief moment, and I imagine him gathering his bearings to start again.

"Dame—"

"He lunged for a photographer, Bianca. What were you thinking going to a place with that much visibility?"

I pinch the bridge of my nose and heave an exasperated sigh. "I know. I'm sorry. Things have just been…" I trail off. I'm not sure what they've been. Crazy? Amazing? *Life-changing?* How can I go back to normal when I know what it feels like to be loved by Jaden?

But before I can finish the rest of my sentence, Damien's voice cuts into my thoughts. "Fake. That's the word you're searching for, B. It's not real. Is it? Can you honestly tell me you want this marriage to work?"

Willing the tears not to fall, I glance up at the ceiling.

"How many times have we watched those reality dating shows? One second they're head over heels, madly in love. Then the show ends."

I swallow, hating the hollow ache in my chest.

"The next thing you know, they pack it up and go back to real life…separately." Damien sighs like it pains him to be the one to burst the bubble we've been living in these past couple of weeks. "There's a reason for that, B. Love takes more than forced proximity, holiday magic, and an accidental marriage. You have to go through real things together…"

My throat tightens and a weight settles on my heart, but I need to hear this. No matter how much I don't want to, I have to let it sink in.

If being in the public eye together proved anything, it's

that Jaden deserves someone he can love without boundaries or impossible tests.

I flit a glance over to my sleeping husband. He's lightly snoring with one leg stretched over the other. His arm is draped over my side of our bed—where I'm supposed to be.

I lower my chin, twisting the diamond ring on my finger.

"Dame, I know the Snowball Jam is in three days…" Slipping the band from my finger, I close my eyes letting the tears stream down my cheeks. The cool metal is hard and heavy in my palm.

"Have the contracts from Museik and the annulment documents ready to sign when I see you."

His sigh is filled with relief.

"Are you sure?" he asks, and I'm stuck by how out of character the question is coming from Damien. He arranged the villa, gave us the gift box, then told me how gullible I am to consider any of it real.

What are you doing to me Dame?

I swipe at my eyes and swallow the emotion thick in my throat. "I'll be staying with Mom for the rest of week. Please have Omar prepare the car and have it ready in fifteen minutes."

He's silent for a beat before we disconnect the call, but my heart is too heavy to overanalyze his angle.

It takes me ten to pack my bags and set them by door. I haven't showered or bothered to get dressed. It seems pointless when I'm just going to lie down to cry in another bed.

Lowering my knee on the mattress, I lean in to lightly touch Jaden's shoulder then I step back.

When his eyes flutter open, he surveys me for a second. Registering my jacket and purse on my shoulder, he rolls onto his back. He scrubs his hands over his face, weaving his fingers through his hair.

"Why?" His voice is barely above a whisper. It's thick with a mix of sleep and emotion, but his tone is hard.

The side of his jaw juts out under the pressure of his clenched teeth.

"Why are you leaving?"

Swiping at my tears, I lower my chin.

"I just can't see how this is going to work, Jaden. I'm about to go on a world tour. I'd never ask you to leave you family or Eric. And how can I ask you to wait for me? Why would you?"

I bite the inside of my cheek, buying myself time.

"How can I, in good conscience, put you guys in the public eye? You'll have no privacy. There'll always be some photographer who thinks he can talk to me any kind of way. Are you going to fight them all?"

The only truth that should matter is how much we love each other, but what if Damien is right? What if outside the villa we don't make it? Will I regret passing on my dream? Will we resent each other?

"So that's it?" His voice thunders, ricocheting off the walls. "We get an annulment and we never see each other again?"

He doesn't even look at me. His stare is empty and distant.

"It doesn't have to be like that. We can still be frien—"

"Don't."

Finally, his eyes snap to mine, his brown irises cold, hard, and flinty. "I'll never be able to be just friends with you, Bianca."

He heaves a frustrated sigh, shaking his head as I sob.

"You don't get it. I'm in *love* with you. Since the day we met I've been drawn to you. I crave you, ache for you." The emotion in his tone squeezes my heart, wrenching agonizing sobs from me.

"I'm sorry. I'm so, so sorry." I cry.

"My heart is set on making a life with you and building a family you. Not right away, but I can't pretend I don't feel all of that just because it'll be in the public eye."

My tears fall freely.

I want all of that, too, with Jaden—the close-knit relationships with our families and friends, the chance to start one of our own in a warm home with our own traditions and photos lining the walls. It occurs to me that I didn't let myself think about it because I never thought it would really happen.

The realization wrecks me to have to choose without any guarantees.

Jaden must see the war between panic and indecision playing on my face because he sits up and angles his body to me. Taking my free hand in his, he searches my eyes, imploring me to give us a chance.

"You're breaking my heart, my reina. Please don't give up on us." His emotion-choked voice reaches down and crushes my heart. "I love you so much, I'm begging you..."

My chest tightens and my pulse quickens. "I love you, too." Through sobs, I shake my head.

"Then stay with me. Build a life with me." He's breathless and desperate as he cups my face in his hands. His big brown eyes boring into me as he kisses me into collusion. "We'll figure everything out together. I promise."

The cracks in my willpower start to spread, and every cell in my body wants to cave. I'm going to give in and take a leap in faith...

But a light rap on the door stops me cold.

"Your car is here, miss." Omar wedges himself in the cracked door, his voice echoing hard and final off the walls.

Blinking back my tears, I open my hand and place Jaden's ring on the nightstand. "I'll never regret marrying you, but I can't see how we can make it work." Turning on my heel, I rush toward Omar.

With one more look over my shoulder at my sweet husband, I let the door slam closed on us.

Later, when I get out of the car. Mom grabs me into one of those bear hugs that make you cry even harder. She's got intuition down to a science. One good look and she has a whole read on a person, which is why she only has to see my puffy eyes and curved shoulders to know I'm crumbling inside over Jaden.

Deep sobs wrack my body, leaving me spent and numb when Mom finally pulls away.

"Tea or hot chocolate?" Mom kisses my head, squeezing once more before making her way into the kitchen.

I plop down in the center of the new couch, pulling my knees into my chest.

Through a sniffle, I opt for hot chocolate with extra whipped cream even though it reminds me of Jaden. I've only just left him, and already I'm hard pressed to find anything that doesn't remind me of him or us. I just want the holidays to be over so I can try to move on. The sooner the reminders are gone—all the trees and wreaths, the ugly sweaters, hot chocolate—the sooner I can pretend my heart isn't broken.

My phone vibrates against my thigh and I jam my hand into my pocket to fish it out, praying it's Jaden.

It's not.

Damien again.

He's called five times, but I don't have the energy or the

heart to talk about work right now. I know it's been less than two weeks since Jaden and I found each other, but it's like the toothpaste is out of the tube. I'm in love. There's no putting my feelings back. They're out, and they'll be with me not matter where in the world the Museik tour takes me.

Setting my phone on the coffee table, I recline, letting my head rest against the back of the sofa.

A few minutes later, Mom slowly enters the living room in her fluffy red slippers carrying her favorite dotted tray with two mugs of steaming-hot cocoa.

"Now. Start from the moment you left the party at the Brooks' until you walked in this door looking like your heart's been ripped out." She sits on the edge of the cream-colored armchair perpendicular to the couch.

I swipe at the dollop of whipped cream with my finger and shove it into my mouth letting the fluffy sweetness dissolve on my tongue.

"I ended it," I blurt out, and the tears immediately return.

"Why?"

"Mom, what do you mean, why?" I feel the heat crawling from my neck to my cheeks. "Obviously, it was never going to work. We got married on a whim at a little chapel downtown by a man dressed as Elvis in red and green crushed velvet. Please tell me what about that screams 'forever' to you?"

Clearing her throat, she nods for me to continue.

"How? How is it supposed to work out between us? I'm going on a world tour. I'll be gone for a year."

Mom purses her lips, and I know this is a shitty way to spring the tour on her, but she wanted all the details.

"Oh, and in case you're not on social media or don't subscribe to all the gossip magazines, Jaden's face is plastered everywhere because he was about to attack a photographer for me…"

"I see."

Throwing my hands up, I heave a sigh of exasperation. "Mom, are you even listening to me? I'm telling you *I'm* used to the spotlight, and I don't want to subject Jaden and his family to it. They have enough worries of their own with Eric's medical bills. Privacy isn't something you just give up on a whim."

"Do you love him?" Mom asks, ignoring everything I've said.

Ugh. See?

"Clearly, you haven't been listening to anything I've said."

She picks up her mug and takes a small sip before wiping the corners of her mouth with a napkin. With dramatic effort, she scoots back in the chair and folds her arms over her chest.

Here we go.

I know this tactic—the one-word answers, answering questions with a question, the silent treatment so I draw my own conclusions before she helps me see the error in my logic. The joke's on her, though, because there is literally no logic to anything that's happened between Jaden and me. *None.*

So there.

As stubborn as she is, Mom forgets I'm a younger version of her. Every tactic in her arsenal of reverse psychology, I've not only *learned* but perfected.

Mirroring her, I scoot further into the couch, crossing my arms and tipping my chin up.

For the first two minutes, I'm good. On the inside, I'm patting myself on the back for not caving. *Or feeling like my heart* is *being ripped out over Jaden*. Quietly, I scrutinize the tiny changes Mom's made around the house. The tree with all the old ornaments we've accumulated over the years on vacations and milestones are there, but she's added a few new ones—a tiny glass of red wine, a prickly pickle, tube of lipstick, a silver heart engraved with the year.

I flit a glance over to her, but she's holding steady, so I move on to the mantle above the fireplace.

Again, the old pictures are there, but my gaze snaps to a new glossy photo of Mom and a man I don't recognize. He's a tall Hispanic man wearing a navy suit to fit his slim frame, and his salt and pepper dark hair is a neatly tapered at the sides. He's good looking for an older guy, but it's Mom who steals the spotlight. Her dark hair is down, and her curls are pulled to one shoulder. She's wearing a simple black dress, but her wine-stained red lips…

This time when I turn to her, I can tell she's been following my line of vision because she whips her eyes back to me at the same time.

"Mom?"

"Yes," she says simply and evenly, as if she hasn't been holding out on me.

She lifts her chin just so, and I know.

It's not glaringly obvious, but the details were all there had I taken the time to look. Her rich brown eyes seem brighter and vibrant when she holds my stare. Her shoulders are pushed back. Her skin glows with pinched pink cheeks like she's blushing, for goodness sake. She's beaming.

My heart pounds in my chest. Even the way her legs are crossed at the ankles is telling. I cannot close my mouth…or blink.

"You're seeing someone." It's not a question.

"Yes."

What the heck?

I gasp as all the air inside me is vacuumed out. "And you didn't think to tell me? Why?"

Her slow blink is another tactic—one of her best. Over the years, I'd looked for the cues to know what she was about to say before she said it, and apparently, it's like riding a bike because I still have it. The eye blink is a nonverbal queue for "smart-ass reply on deck."

Sure enough, she doesn't disappoint.

"Because you didn't ask."

"Seriously? That's not something you think you should have volunteered to your only daughter?"

Mom picks up her mug. "When would I have had the opportunity, Bianca? Since you got back to Vegas, you've been gone with the girls, you got married, hid away with your husband in a secret villa, partied with your in-laws, and only now have come home...with a broken heart, I might add."

It's not a smart-ass reply.

It's the truth, which is always the harder pill to swallow.

I open my mouth and close it again, feeling blindsided. What was I expecting? Why did I assume Mom was going to stay single for the rest of her life? Because Dad is gone? She's had her turn and that's it for her?

Do I need her to be frozen in time?

Deep down, I think part of me does. I know it's selfish. With her stuck in the past, at least someone hasn't changed on me or left me. But the other half of me wants her to find real happiness, human connection, and a chance to run away from all the darkness of the past.

"Mom." My voice is little more than a whisper.

Squeezing my eyes closed, I shake my head and pinch

the bridge of my nose. How could I be so self-consumed? *Why didn't I notice?*

"I'm sorry," I say, opening my eyes again. "I'm happy for you."

"Oh, come on, now. You're not yet, but you will be." She chuckles and I laugh-cry with her. "I don't blame you, though. It was the hardest thing we've been through, losing Daddy. You've sort of counted on me to be your anchor to the past so you can hold on without having to get close."

My tears stream freely, and I don't fight them.

"Baby, we can't move forward in life if we're always looking in the rearview mirror. Ever since Daddy died in that accident, you've been running, holding people at a distance. It's time to stop." She leans forward and passes me a tissue. "I'm not replacing him, honey. I'm living while I'm here."

I blot at the corners of my eyes with the tissue, but the tears keep spilling over the way they always do when I think about Mom getting older.

"Holding on tight to the people who matter... That's what I want for you," Mom murmurs.

"I know."

"But do you? Bianca, you don't have to know *how* things will work out, you just have to have *faith* that they will."

My phone pings again, and my shoulders tense. My heart skitters to a stop.

If it's Jaden, I still don't know what I'll say. I just...I miss him.

My eyes dart from my phone on the coffee table to Mom, who nods indicating for me to check the message. She knows the uneasy anticipation of waiting every time the phone rings or pings or buzzes and how the heart stutters.

As soon as I peek at the screen, my shoulders sag. The message is short and to the point, though.

Damien Eisner 7:02pm
The casino upped their offer.

My eyebrows knit together and the wheels in my head get to turning.

The handful of words roll around the back of my mind. I can't discount how my hopes lift slightly as Damien's earlier question comes flooding back. *Are you sure?* He's full of advice and opinions but he never questions my decisions.

Was he testing me? Checking to see if I know what I want?

He's like Mom in that way, with his riddles.

The man spent the morning convincing me love takes more than forced proximity, holiday magic, and an accidental marriage. But haven't Jaden and I gone through real things together?

We were at the villa, but it was real.

Sometimes, I wish people would just come out and say what they mean instead of leaving me to figure things out on my own.

I narrow my eyes and chew on my bottom lip.

Dame and I had talked about the casino residency a few times, but he never stressed it as a viable option for my career. It had always been about the world tour, and how perfect it would be because I didn't have any attachments or ties back home. Being gone a year on buses and planes without someone tethering your heartstrings to a post, it seemed easier…

I lift my chin, sowing a small seed of hope in my heart.

When I meet Mom's questioning gaze, I don't have to tell

her I'm working through all the possibilities to follow both my dreams and my heart.

"Let me guess, faith found a way?" she asks.

A silly smile quirks the corners of my lips.

Apparently, the silent treatment tactic is still effective. I've been beating myself up trying to choose between going off on a world tour and leaving my family, friends, and the only man I've ever loved behind or passing on a once-in-a-lifetime career opportunity and possibly ending up resenting Jaden. *Awesome choices.*

How was I supposed to know there was a third option?

I've got to start paying better attention to the people in my life.

CHAPTER TEN

For the second time today, *It's A Wonderful Life* is playing on the big screen in my parents' living room. If I have to hear Dad enunciate "an angel gets his *wings*" to Eric one more time, I'm going to just get up and leave. Forget Christmas Eve and the family countdown. This is not what I had in mind at all when I wanted to take my mind off Bianca.

"Jaden, please tell your brother to clean his ears. He's thick-headed. It's *wings*. He keeps going about *sings*." Dad throws his hands up, but I catch a glimpse of Eric's smirk, and I have to laugh.

It's not so much their bickering as it is the subject matter that's funny. Even in my own family's house, I can't escape Bianca. Monday back at the villa, she'd had contagious giggles, replaying this same argument.

On the television, the movie cuts to commercial, and there she is in an ad for the Snowball Jam. Bianca is on stage, her voice filling the air as she sings her number-one Christmas song, "Mistletoe Memories."

I scrub my hands over my face and groan.

"Is it the Christmas Crunch because I've been feeling a little rumble in the jungle myself." Eric shudders playfully, always the comic relief. "This too shall pass."

Eric and Dad laugh at my brother's ornery jokes.

"On that note, I think I'll go see if the ladies need my help." I shake my head, still laughing as I stand and take easy strides to the kitchen.

Three pairs of eyes snap to me. In a very effective intimidation tactic, Mom, Aunt Sarah, and Denise each wipe their hands on their respective hand towels. Folding their arms over their chests, the message is clear: I have some explaining to do. *Not that I know what that is at the moment...*

"What did I do?" I ask, having been on the receiving end of this all-female iron curtain before. I'm frozen in the doorway, unwilling to move. "That was Dad and Eric arguing in the other room. I was just sitting there."

Denise rolls her eyes followed by Aunt Sarah, but Mom lowers her chin in a way that could only mean *don't cross me.* In other words, tell them everything about the one subject I was hoping to avoid. Bianca.

"Fine. What do you want to know? It's over."

"Why?" Aunt Sarah pries.

I blow out a frustrated breath. "Can I at least get a slice of turkey if I have to stand here while you interrogate me?"

Mom purses her lips but relents and forks a piece of juicy dark meat from the leg. Handing me the fork, she plants a fist on her hip. "Now, why didn't you fight harder for her?"

The fork is in my mouth. The salty spices and warm flavors are on my tongue, but I have to stop myself from spitting it out. "Fight harder? Why do you all assume I didn't fight for her? She's the one who left. She said she couldn't see how we could make this work."

Shaking my head, I set the fork with the once-delicious meat fully intact onto the counter. I've lost my appetite.

"This is really what you guys have been in here doing? Drawing all the wrong conclusions? Meanwhile, my heart is in pieces."

The three of them are ridiculous in their frilly Christmas blouses and elf aprons. Santa's little helpers, indeed. They toss around pointed stares between them, shifting this way and that, communicating in some secret woman language.

When they turn to me, I shrug. My eyebrows shoot up.

Naturally, the mouthpiece, Denise, is the first to talk. "So, she didn't say she didn't love you?" She cocks her head, ready to scrutinize my physical reaction and overanalyze my answer.

"Nooo." I drag the word out, considering where they're going with this line of questioning. "That's the one part we agree on. We care about each other, but right after the Snowball Jam, she's leaving…going on tour."

Aunt Sarah presses at a loose black strand out of her eye. "Go with her. Do something wild for once in your sappy life."

My eyes widen, and my mouth falls open. Of all the things I imagined she was going to say, "leave" was clear at the bottom of the list. A flush of adrenaline tingles through my body, and a fluttery feeling whips through my stomach.

Her star is shining so bright. What if having me around only dims her light?

"I can't…there's no way I can just leave. You're my family. You guys need me."

They shake their heads in a synchronized move that reminds me of the three good fairies from *Sleeping Beauty.*

I let out a nervous bark of laughter. *Have they suddenly*

forgotten how much we need each other? "Wh-what about Eric?" I stammer.

"What about me?" Eric wheels himself onto the tile then rotates his chair so he's taken a clear alignment with the women. He lifts his head, baring his throat and there is no humor tugging at his laugh lines. "What did you mean?"

Letting my chin drop to my chest, I close my eyes. "I just meant that I want to be here with you." My jaw is tight when I meet his gaze again. "If anything happened to you and I wasn't here... I'd never forgive myself."

All my worst fears rush to the surface—losing Eric, the devastation to our family unit. Life would never be the same.

A small smile dances over his lips. "This disease has taken so many things from me...from us. Please don't let it be the reason you don't live your life."

I blink, letting my head fall back to keep the tears at baby.

"J, we know how much you love us and everything you do for us, but we still have each other. That's what family does, we fight for each other." He pauses for a beat. "All I'm saying is, if you feel at all that Bianca could be a part of this family, you have to fight for her."

When I lower my head, the women have surrounded Eric in solidarity, but their expressions have softened toward me.

Denise picks the fork up off the counter and stretches it out to me. "Here. It's Christmas Eve. Eat and be merry. You and Bianca love each other. All the other stuff is just background noise." She tosses me a half-smile. "Together we'll help you figure out a way to hear the music even if you have to follow her around the globe."

"You know..." Dad appears, slapping an arm over my shoulder and tinkling a jingle bell tied to the mistletoe above our head with his free hand. He plants a big one on my cheek and I flash him a playful grimace.

But then his face lights up. "Your brother may be right, yet. Every time a bell rings, a pop star *sings*..."

I stare at him in confusion.

"Tomorrow is Christmas Day. Won't she be at the Snowball Jam?"

I nod, sensing where he's going with this line of reasoning. "Maybe *we* should help you fight the good fight."

I have a sneaking suspicion that in addition to helping me win Bianca back, Dad might have an ulterior motive. As a movie buff, he's always wanted to participate in a grand gesture. The fact that it'll be Christmas *and* he'll get to pretend he's part of Bedford Falls coming together to validate George Bailey's life... Well, what a wonderful life it will be.

The next day, instead of singing carols and falling into a turkey coma to the tune of Clarence getting his wings, my entire family is on edge. We're counting down the hours to the Snowball Jam. I've made the phone calls to Damien, who surprisingly, is on board with my plan. We've got VIP tickets and backstage passes. After the second song, when Bianca is between costume changes, that's when it's all supposed to go down.

For now, I'm on my second spiked eggnog to ease my nerves.

"You're sure you don't want to go with something a little more dashing or debonair? A tux?" Aunt Sarah stretches her bright red lips into a curious smile.

The ugly sweaters are back, and she and Denise have been vying for anything else to wear since there's a high likelihood we could be televised. Or worse, turned into a meme on social media.

Quirking a smile at them, I offer the only other solution. "If you don't want to be a part of this, I'll understand," I say, sensing they'd rather take the risk than miss out on a sold-out concert in a stadium that seats thousands. *Anyway, this could be the day they get discovered…*

When the driver arrives to pick us up two hours later, my nerves are all over the place. The closer we get to the arena, the more real it feels and the closer I am to knowing how the rest of my life will turn out.

Mom reaches for my hand, takes it in her warm, velvety one, and squeezes.

"Maybe I'm a little old-fashioned, but I saw the way you two were together. She had that look in her eye women get only when they're in love. Time, space, and distance can't erase it." She flits a warm glance over at Dad before returning her gaze to me. "We dated for years, but I knew I wanted to marry your father the second I laid eyes on him."

I lift our hands and kiss the back of hers. "Thanks, Mom."

"She'd be crazy to let you get away."

STILL REELING FROM MOM'S LITTLE TALK AND THE NOISE LEVEL of the arena, I can barely stand still backstage. At every turn, there are dancers, makeup artists, and crew dressed in all black. They're all so busy, running around like chickens with their heads cut off, so we've been moved to a small room off the stage where I'm still trying to decide what my grand profession of love is going to look and sound like.

We can't just stand there in the middle of the stage and expect her to take me back just because we're wearing ugly sweaters and asking her to love me in front tens of thousands of people. *Can we?*

No.

My heart skitters when a voice on the walkie-talkie says, "Bianca to the stage." *Shit.*

It has to be something along the lines of, "I love you. Don't divorce me. I'll follow you to the ends of the earth," but more romantic.

On a small screen displaying the stage, I wait with my heart in my throat to see her. Then the lights go down. The crowd erupts into excited screams and shrieks. Then, the first playful notes of "Tinsel on the Tree" waft through the air.

A spotlight beams down on her in a frilly green dress.

"Oh, now, doesn't she look beautiful," Mom says.

Aunt Sarah and Denise hum their agreement.

"Twinkling lights. All those nights. It's only this time of year when I see…"

Bianca is more beautiful than I remember, playing to her fans as she dances to the beat. In the moment, every desperate fiber of my being knows I could never move on without knowing what would have happened if I'd tried to win her back. I feel irrational because I'm willing to do anything, even travel the world to be with her.

A manic energy courses through my veins as her first number ends.

Again, the walkie-talkie squawks something I can't quite make out.

The crew member who's been assigned to us turns to me. "She's going to go back on the stage in two minutes. We'll move you to the wing where you'll wait for the song to be over. She won't be able to see you, but when I give you the cue, you'll have less than a minute to get in position."

I nod. "Got it."

The mic crackles to life, and then Bianca, who'd twirled off stage, reappears in a glittering red gown. She tucks a long curl behind her ear and blows the audience a kiss.

Fifteen minutes later, when we're guided onto the stage to our mark and the curtain goes up, I'm certain I don't have it. My heart jackhammers against my chest as the six of us stare out at a sea of restless people trying to figure out who the ugly sweater family is and why we're interrupting the concert.

But then, the first voice yells out. "It's him! Jaden Brooks."

A collection of gasps sweeps over the crowd, followed by murmurs of "the husband," "the Rideo driver," and requests to "marry me."

They're rooting for me...

My pulse revs up, and I stand a little taller.

Our guy from the crew gives us the signal for "one minute" and I can't hear anything over the sound of my heartbeat pounding in my ears. Fumbling to get Grandmas' ring out of my pocket, I finally pinch it between my fingers and hold it up for the crowd.

They go wild, chanting, "Marry her!"

I'm so focused on the force of thousands of people pumping me up, the energizing feeling of adrenaline zipping through my veins, I miss our cue. When the crowd falls silent, I turn to see Bianca step on stage.

"Jaden?"

Her shiny eyes are wide as her gaze darts from me to my family to her Mom and Damien who've joined us on stage for the good fight. Even Margo and Cara have joined forces with us.

I take a deep breath, trying to ignore the microphone the

guy pinned to my snowflake sweater. "Bianca." My voice echoing over the arena startles me. I swallow. "I'm here. *We're* here to ask…"

She laughs through her tears as our family aligns themselves behind me the way we practiced. "What's on your mind?"

Laughter rumbles over the audience.

"If you're not too busy…" I trail off playing to the crowd to buy myself some time. Then I clear my throat as the crew member taps his watch. "Will you—"

"Oh, heck. Will you marry us…marry him?" Aunt Sarah cuts me off, posing for the camera with puckered lips.

Bianca pulls her lower lip between her teeth, laughing through her tears. "Yes. I'll marry all of you," she announces to the tune of thousands of cheers and whistles.

"I'll go with you on tour or move to L.A. I don't care where we live, I just want to be with my wife."

A megawatt smile stretches over her face, and her watery eyes sparkle under the lights as we meet in the middle of the stage. I band my arms around her, inhaling her warmth and sweet scent as I seek and find her lips. "I love you so much."

"I love you, too."

Chants erupt, and the noise is music to my ears. "She said 'yes!' She said 'yes!'"

I can hardly believe it myself, but I'm okay with the direction our new adventure is taking. This is just the beginning. No matter where we are, we'll be with our families in our hearts.

Bianca pulls away and lifts the microphone to her mouth. "Merry Christmas, Las Vegas! We're going to be seeing a lot more of each other when I start my residency at the Coeur Hotel and Casino on The Strip next year."

She meets my gaze. "Let's be where the people we love are."

I nod, brushing my lips over hers and cover my microphone. "I might've made an appointment with a realtor, just in case. There's a beautiful home with double garages and a circular driveway not too far from my family with a for sale sign on it."

Our families join us as the music starts. We dance and sing along to "Jingle Bell Rock" as a sea of Bianca's fans help us celebrate.

Later when the Jumbotron illuminates as Bianca hits the beginning notes of her Christmas anthem, "Mistletoe Memories," the arena goes even wilder. It's loud and raucous as they sing along. The place is filled with Christmas cheer.

"Mistletoe memories of just us *two*." Bianca throws her head back to belt out the last word before turning to serenade me in the wings. "Baby, no matter the season, I love you."

She's staying.

It's not just for me, but for her dreams and our future. I'm so fortunate to help make a few of them come true.

As the song fades and "I'll Be Home for Christmas" begins, I watch my wife bask in the light, and I'm already nostalgic for the holidays, the places we'll go, and the family we'll make. I can't imagine our future being any brighter.

NOW HIRING FREELANCE WRITERS
THE GRAPEVINE
THE SNOWBALL JAM
SNOWBALL JAM
CHRISTMAS DAY
WITH BIANCA
Winter Wonderland
DOWNTOWN LAS VEGAS

SHE SAID "YES" AGAIN
Merry Christmas
From our family to yours
BIANCA AND JADEN
MARRIED
&BRIGHT
WELCOME HOME BIANCA
Get all the details about Bianca's new residency at the Coeur Hotel and Casino.
Plus, exclusive scoop on where Jaden's realtor says they're looking to buy.
ALL THE REASONS WHY WE LOVE BIANCA AND JADEN

Thank you for spending your time with Bianca and Jaden. If you enjoyed Married & Bright, please consider leaving a *review* on **Goodreads** or your favorite online retailer.

Keep reading for an excerpt from
Mingle All the Way.
See what a serious (-ly fake) holiday office romance is like…

Join me in my reader group. I'd love to chat! That's where I connect with readers most.
Mia Heintzelman Reader Group

CHAPTER 1

"Have ye no fear. She has arrived!" I sing, twirling over to my best friend, co-worker, and general event planning badass who's standing at a table at the back of the room. Nina is petite—barely up to my shoulder—and her thick, dark brown hair is in a perky ponytail. She's completely adorable. Also, I would do anything for her.

"Where do you need me? I brought a stopwatch—" I give the top button a click. It's responding ping is about as chipper as I am. "Just in case, I also brought my game face. This is Vegas. We can't be too careful."

Her perfectly micro-bladed brows dance as she gives me a quick once-over from my fabulous black thigh-high boots to my fierce red shift dress.

"*Yesss.*" She draws the word out, matching my dramatics with a snap of her fingers.

Nina darts her sparkly brown eyes over my shoulder as she tucks a glossy chestnut strand behind her ear. She leans in for a cheek-to-boob hug. Her cheek, my boob. *She's fun-*

sized. I'm somewhere in between leggy volleyball player and WNBA player, though I am horizontally challenged. But, I digress.

I'm not here for men.

Just because I sell happily-ever-afters for the Lovestruck dating app doesn't mean it's a guaranteed employee benefit.

"She *is* ready. Red lips will do it every time," Nina continues.

"Bliss & Makeup Co. This is Crimson Queen," I say, filling her in on the best makeup to hit melanated girls since…ever. "Do yourself a favor and get one." I pucker, give her a shoulder shimmy and toss her a sweet smile.

She knows I'm not here to play around with these fools. This lipstick is all the drama allowed tonight.

"Girl, I've got this. Eight minutes sharp…like clock-work." I click the stopwatch button again for effect then whip my faux locs over my shoulder to the long line of bistro tables with flickering candles. Giant red Mylar heart balloons are strung with mistletoe over each two-seater table. "I'll usher the singles in. You'll do your little spiel, then the timed dates start. After, they'll have thirty minutes to mingle and fill out their little 'Let's make sparks' cards before I shuffle them out into the hands of the press for interviews."

I have a megawatt smile and arch a brow at her like, *they aren't even ready for all this, here.*

Nina's face twists with concern.

"What? You think they need more than half an hour to mingle?" I ask, failing to see the error in my plan.

It's the weekend after Thanksgiving. Technically, it's Small Business Saturday. No one is going to do anything to mess up the fat bonus coming my way when Nina pulls this event off. My plan is foolproof. Everyone who's anyone in

Vegas is talking about it, and the PR companies are set to dutifully rave about it. When they do, ad sales on Cyber Monday will shoot through the roof, and Spencer James will be so thrilled, he'll gift everyone at Lovestruck financial tokens of his appreciation.

It's a no-brainer.

So, tonight there will be speed dating at this Lovestruck signature Mix'n'Mingle, but I will also duck and dive in and out of shadows to ensure things go off without a hitch.

When Nina doesn't verbalize what's screwing her face into a panic-stricken mess, my Spidey senses go off.

"Seriously, what?" I ask again. "Are you nervous? Did some guy already corner you? Because—"

"No. Nothing like that..." Nina's voice dies off, and I'm slightly relieved. These dating events can be dangerous for women in the game.

I don't know where men drew this conclusion, but for some reason, they think we're like some hyper-sexualized beings who love it when sleazy people aggressively "flirt" or demand reasons why we *shockingly,* don't want a second date.

Yeah, we love it when you make us feel unsafe in the name of love.

I have nothing against policing a bunch of people scheming for Christmas party plus-ones this time of year, but some people need to learn how to keep it classy.

That's what I'm here for.

"Actually..." Nina continues.

I busy myself tugging at the hem of my dress. I'm only halfway listening now because I've spotted the festive-looking open bar—my other excuse for showing up at a work event on my off day.

"Riley," Nina says my name flatly, which gets my attention.

"Yeah?"

"Change of plans. I need you in a *slightly* different capacity…" Her tense smile looks like it might snap at any second.

"Okaaay…" I drag the word out as I cock my head and narrow my gaze.

"Uh…" She scrunches her freckled nose and peeks an eye open. She's literally shaking in her open-toe booties. "The host from the speed-dating company has got all this stuff covered, so I don't actually need you to help *with* the speed dates. I need you to *be* a speed date."

See? I should've known this was too good to be true. My shoulders sag, and my head falls back as I groan. "What the heck, Nina? You know how I feel about dating in general. What makes you think I want to go on a dozen eight-minute dates all in one night? That's ninety-six excruciating minutes of hell for me. You do realize that, right?"

She sighs, and her big, pleading, puppy dog eyes land on me with full force. "It's the holidays," she whines. "You won't have to do the mingle part or the interviews. Two people canceled, and I don't have an even number for the rotations."

This time it's me who sighs—a massive, throaty, full chest heave. Then my thoughts snag on the first part of that sentence. *Two people.*

"Wait." My posture is ramrod straight now. I square my body to Nina and lean down to meet her eyes. "Who else did you get to fill in?"

No sooner is the question out of my mouth when I have my answer.

Chase Campbell from web development bounds through the double doors with a cocky half-grin and perfectly groomed beard. He looks like he ripped his fashion sense right out *GQ's* Best-Dressed Men of the Week—the Irish edition. He's tall, muscly, and lean with carefree product-whipped red hair. He's also incredibly annoying because he knows he's gorgeous. *Ugh.* Of their own accord, my eyes take in his cuffed dark jeans and perfectly rumpled military-style green jacket, which I'm guessing is his version of no-fuss casual.

There's nothing subtle about the man wearing the prep-meets-free-spirit clothes, though.

Which is why I always ignore him.

Quickly, I avert my gaze and resort to fidgeting with my cuticles. I'm not part of the Chase Campbell fan club. I leave that to the girls in the marketing department.

Holidays or not, I'm not about to switch it up.

<hr>

"ALL RIGHT. SO, WHERE DO YOU NEED ME? I ASK.

Nina York flashes me a nervous smile. "Thank you so much for coming on such short notice, Chase. I'm totally going to owe you one." She shifts her body away from Riley Mills, whose tight red smile is fraying around the edges.

"Really. It's no problem. I'm happy to help," I say. I swear I hear a snort come from Riley, so reluctantly I tilt my head to meet Riley's steely gaze, careful not to gawk. "Hey, Riley."

She's tall with sculpted curves, long, shiny locs, and rich, dark skin. She's stunning in a way that always leaves me feeling blindsided, but she's also a serious suit in the most severe sense of the word—all day, every day. She doesn't even take off her jacket at the office despite the casual environment at the Lovestruck headquarters. At first, I thought it was because the A/C is always on high, but someone told me she lives by the "dress for the position you want" motto. Tonight, she must be throwing all that to the wind. The bare skin of her thighs that shows under the hem of her dress to the top of her boots…

The sight makes my stomach clench and sends a jolt right down to my dick.

Down, Chase. Barking up the wrong tree, here.

I swallow and avert my gaze because the reality is, I'm probably the last person Riley Mills expected to see tonight. I can tell the surprise isn't a welcome one.

The Lovestruck office is an open-air industrial building with strategically clumped cubicles meant to section off departments. She's in sales near event planning and marketing at the front of the building, and I'm in IT and web development way in the back by the emergency exit, which I've contemplated using on more than one occasion— anything to avoid passing her desk and the inevitable pursed-lip death stare she seems to reserve just for me.

Not that I have any clue why…

Even if it always looks like it kills her, we try to exchange minimal words—real gems like "hi," "hello," and "thanks for holding the door," which is usually growled. Other than those rare pleasantries, she seems to loathe me for reasons I'm still unaware. For her part, I suspect she interacts with me out of courtesy and professionalism, mostly. For me, it's a combination of fear and self-preservation, which is why I avoid her like the beautiful, bronze goddess plague that she is to my ego.

Nina clears her throat and flashes Riley a pointed stare. In an unexpected twist, Riley says, "Hi." It's like pulling teeth.

Now that wasn't so hard, was it?

Nina bounces up on her toes, breaking up the whole three-word conversation.

"So…" she rests her hands on my shoulders and lowers her chin before blurting out. "I need you to be one of the speed daters."

Oh, fuck. Why?

My gaze slides to Riley who crosses her arms over her chest and shakes her head. Right, she's been asked to be a date, too. So, somewhere in the rotation, Riley and I will be face to face for eight minutes.

In my book, that's plenty of time to get to the bottom of her apparent hatred for me.

Thanks, Nina.

"Yeah, I'm good. Whatever you need," I say with a shrug, doing my best to sound breezy and unaffected. On the inside, however, I'm rubbing my hands together at this twisted conspiracy Nina cooked up for us.

Or did she? Why would she?

Precisely ten minutes later, Nina and some young kid she has doing her gopher work let the singles in, and she gives her perky introduction speech, which is a bubbly welcome and thank you. Then she gives the rules of the event along with a warning about what would constitute dismissal from this event and all future events put on by Lovestruck. *Whoa, I guess she's not messing around.*

Half an hour later, I'm three dates in, two away from Riley, and I catch her sneaking glances over at me. I shoot her a confused look in return. That earns me a smile, which only makes my anticipation of our eight minutes together that much stronger.

Then, we're one table apart. She's with a typical tall, dark, and tattooed guy who is talking about his fitness training business, and I am with a raven-haired CEO who keeps going on about washi tape. *Whatever that is.* Much to my relief, Riley looks bored out of her mind.

When the timer goes off, and I switch into the chair in front of Riley, I go for it. "Want to tell me why you've been giving me the evil eye since date two?" I ask. *Oh, yeah, I'm going for it.*

She shakes her head and smiles. Maybe it's the candlelight flickering off her rich brown skin, or the way it glints off her eyes and turns them a warm shade of amber, but I'm mesmerized. I'm charmed by the prospect of graduating to two-word exchanges.

"Why are you even here? Isn't one of the marketing girls free tonight?" she asks with an eye roll.

Okay, a whole string of words. We're getting somewhere.

"Is that why you hate me?"

She presses a finger to her temple and massages like talking to me is *so* stressful. "Oh, your ego isn't massive or anything. Relax. Not everything is about you, believe me. I was just commenting on our work prospects. That's all." She presses the air with her palms.

There's something telling about the way she keeps looking away.

"Maybe, you don't hate me…because you like me." I cock my head to read her reaction.

"I don't date. Period."

So, you agree. You do like me.

I nod, and the corners of my mouth tug downward as my lower lip protrudes. "Wow. So, what's this we're doing?" I lean in, forcing her gaze, and whisper, "It sort of feels like a date."

She parts her lips then closes them again.

"Just the facts." I shrug and lean back against my chair.

"I'm here as a favor to Nina just like you are, so save it.

And there are free drinks. Don't go reading more into it." She runs a hand over the long black coiled strands of her hair. Then she surprises me. "I don't care how many minutes each date is, it's just nice to see a familiar face and have an unscripted conversation."

"So, you agree. It's nice to see my face…" I'm bobbing my head, biting back a shit-eating grin as a warm, musical laugh pipes out of her. I love this new unexpected banter between us. It's like we've been in the middle of a conversation all this time, and we've just jumped back in where we left off.

Then, the host, a tall, boisterous woman in a black jumpsuit with short platinum-blonde hair eases up to our table and positions the mic inches from her neon pink lips. "I want to pause for a few seconds. Go ahead. Stop the clock!" She gestures to Nina, who is all too happy to hear what the woman has to say.

The host flips the mic between Riley and me. "What are your names?"

We both hesitate, but eventually cave and tell her.

"Now, I don't mean to put you on the spot…" *Oh, sure you do.* "But I want everyone to stop what they're doing and take a look at Chase and Riley. They just met, what, four minutes and twenty-three seconds ago? Just like you. But I'll tell you a little secret. These two…they have it."

The room erupts into applause. Every pair of eyes in the place is on us. Honestly, I'm right there with this woman's assessment. She's not lying. The hair on my arms and the nape of my neck is raised. My heart is fluttering in my chest. I'm aching to reach across and touch Riley…or for her to touch me.

A slow smile tugs at the corners of my mouth until I see

Riley's expression. She's tense. Her eyes dart to the host before landing—hard as bricks—on me.

"When the clock is ticking," the host continues, putting us directly on the spot despite the murder in Riley's eyes, "you can't get to know a person by asking their favorite color and what they do for a living. Questionnaires do not a connection make. You have to jump all the way in. These two are in each other's face, asking questions, smiling—I'm talking fierce eye contact, hair-touching, lips parted, leaning in. Yes, to all of it! The heat between these two is combustible."

In exactly this moment, I realize three fundamental truths. One, by the intensity of Riley's reaction, whatever this loathe-hate thing is, the feelings between us aren't one-sided. Two, the ache to touch her has spread to the growing hard-on in my pants. And three, the pursed-lip death stare is going to be epic on Monday.

ACKNOWLEDGMENTS

Happy holly merry days. Thanks for going along on this ride with me. Hopefully, you snuggled up with a warm cup of something cheery and whizzed through Riley and Chase's story. That you chose my book in which to spend your time is my honor.

This time of year when the season officially changes and we make memories with family is my favorite. Thank you to my husband, Daniel Heintzelman, who has allowed me to leap because he's my net, supporting me.

Shout-outs, hoots, and hollers to my writing family, my IG family, the librarians, bookstagrammers, bloggers, and reviewers. Thank you for enjoying and sharing my story.

To my editors, Danielle and Danylle, I'm indebted to your polishing skills.

Big hugs and smoochie kisses to my family and friends. You are the petals on my flowering tree and the frame holding up my house. You understand and support me even though I'm always with my nose stuck in a book or with my fingers glued to a keyboard spinning tales.

As always, Mommy and Daddy, I love that I'm equally introverted bookworm and (semi-)social butterfly. Thank you for always cheering me on.

My sister, Melissa DeGrazia, let's keep leaping in faith together!

Finally, to my two daughters and my nieces and nephews, I hope my daring pursuit of greatness is inspiration and wind beneath your wings.

Mia Heintzelman is a polka-dot-wearing, horror movie lover, who always has a book and a to-do list in her purse. When she isn't busy writing fictional happily-ever-afters, she is likely reading, or playing board games and eating sweets with her husband and two children. She writes fun, unforgettable, more than just laughs romance about strong women and men with enough heart to fall for them.

Website:

miaheintzelman.com

Subscribe to Mia's Newsletter:
miaheintzelman.com/newsletter.html

Join Mia's FB Reader Group:
Facebook.com/groups/2219575585012649/

facebook.com/miaheintzelmanauthor
twitter.com/miaheintzelman
instagram.com/miaheintzelmanauthor
goodreads.com/miaheintzelman
bookbub.com/authors/miaheintzelman
amazon.com/author/miaheintzelman

www.ingramcontent.com/pod-product-compliance
Lightning Source LLC
Chambersburg PA
CBHW021201110726
47900CB00002B/678